"Ben and Claudia are splitsville!"

"And that means," the cheerleaders practically gushed in unison, "that Ben is wide open for snagging!"

They were too busy jumping up and down over their own potential chances to pay me any mind. Which was a good thing because my heart was doing serious somersaults in my chest. And I knew one look at my burning face would have spilled the beans on my secret crush. Ben Donovan was *free*! I started to tingle from the roots of my auburn hair to the tips of my toes.

But as I looked around at the competition, their slim, perfect bodies slipping effortlessly into their size five cheerleading outfits, and then glanced down at my own chubby body, stuffed into my dumpy uniform, I had to ask: *who am I kidding?*

In my wildest dreams, how could I possibly stand a chance with Ben against these girls?

His. Hers. Theirs.

Snag Him!

GRETCHEN GREENE

BANTAM BOOKS
NEW YORK • TORONTO • LONDON • SYDNEY • AUCKLAND

RL: 6, AGES 012 AND UP

SNAG HIM!
A Bantam Book / April 2001

Cover photography by Barry Marcus.

*Produced by 17th Street Productions,
an Alloy Online, Inc. company.
33 West 17th Street
New York, NY 10011.*

ISBN: 0-553-49371-X

Visit us on the Web! www.randomhouse.com/teens

Published simultaneously in the United States and Canada

*Bantam Books is an imprint of Random House Children's Books, a
division of Random House, Inc. BANTAM BOOKS and the rooster
colophon are registered trademarks of Random House, Inc. Bantam Books,
1540 Broadway, New York, New York 10036.*

PRINTED IN THE UNITED STATES OF AMERICA

OPM   0 9 8 7 6 5 4 3 2 1

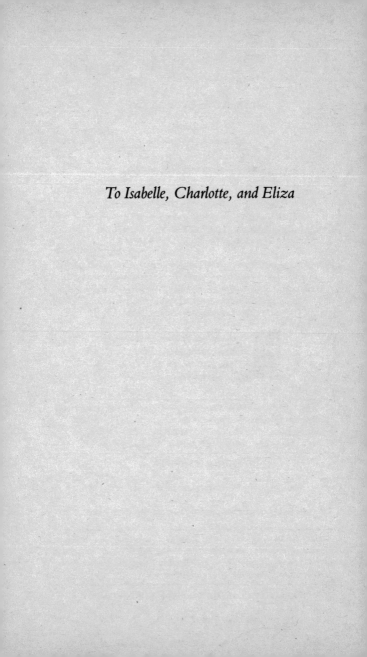

To Isabelle, Charlotte, and Eliza

One

Megan

*D*on't look, Megan! Avert your eyes! The warning bells rang in my head. *Uh-oh—too late . . .* Megan Kennedy, the chubby girl staring back at me from the locker-room mirror, was too big to miss. I looked away, yanking up my long athletic socks and lacing my cleats. But no matter how I tried, I couldn't shake the image—or ignore my bare chubby thighs— as I worked on my footwear.

Get a grip! I scolded myself. *Your lacrosse team is about to play in the division championship.* As captain of the Hartley Cyclones, I had to stay upbeat. The last thing my teammates needed was for my weight issues to mess up our game.

I smoothed down my brand-new purple-and-gold-striped jersey and sneaked another peek at my reflection. Sort of like those rubberneckers who can't keep their eyes off a highway wreck. *Yep, I'm still here,* the chubette seemed to say. *Still sporting that extra twenty pounds.* I slammed my locker shut and resolutely turned my back on the mirror.

"Hey, Megs! Ready to lead us to victory?"

A welcome voice snapped me out of my weight-induced psychosis. I smiled as my teammate and friend, Serena Jefferson, came bounding toward me, a big grin stretched across her pretty, dark-skinned face.

Of my two best friends, Serena Jefferson and Laurie Holmes, Serena was the one I most wanted to be like. She might be a few pounds overweight according to some doctor's chart, but she was cool with her body. No weight issues there. And she dated. She was between boyfriends at the moment, but out of choice, not because no one wanted her. And not because she *thought* no one wanted her or *could* want her. Laurie, even though she was rail thin, was more like me—somewhere between the warthog and the dung beetle on the self-confidence scale.

I gave an exaggerated tug at my jersey and shook it in Serena's direction. "More like I'm going to crash and burn. I feel like the Goodyear Blimp in these stripes. Couldn't they at least be running up and down?"

"Megs!" Serena placed an admonishing hand on her hip. "Some girls have bad-hair days—you have bad-*body* days. Are you still smarting over that English paper?"

2

"Ugh," I groaned. "Why'd you have to bring that up?"

Serena opened the locker next to mine and tossed in her backpack. "It's obvious. Something goes wrong somewhere in your life, and you immediately start moaning about your weight." She pulled off her tie-dyed T-shirt and slipped on her Cyclone jersey.

"I *am* fat," I insisted, "whether Miss Pine gave me a lousy B—a B!" I cried, "Or not."

Serena crossed her arms, looking at me with one raised eyebrow. "Uh-huh?"

I tugged at a thread on my purple gym shorts. "Okay, so maybe I wouldn't feel so bad if she'd given me a better grade. But I worked hard on that paper. I was expecting at least an A-minus if not an A!"

Serena pushed her dark, tightly twisted hair off her face and wrapped it in a ponytail. "So what happened?"

"I don't know." A rush of air escaped from between my lips. "I didn't have a chance to read her comments. I thought I'd wait until there're no sharp objects handy."

Serena rolled her eyes, stifling a laugh. "Megs, you're too much. Forget about it. *Seriously.* Without you Lincoln is going to trounce us. And I want that trophy." She stood staring at me for a moment. "And you are *not* fat. Now, I'm going to get our sticks. Be in a winning mood when I get back. Or else."

I grinned despite myself. Besides my dad, Serena was the only person in my life who couldn't care less about my weight. Even my mom, who was always telling me what a cute figure I had, couldn't stop stocking the coffee table with magazines featuring diet articles. As if I hadn't already tried every diet known to mankind—and failed.

I took a breath. *Okay, so I'm overweight.* Was that the end of the world? It shouldn't be, right? The problem was my weight seemed to intrude on everything else in my life. Especially the romance department. There I was, sixteen years old, and I'd never been on a real date with a guy, let alone shared a kiss or held hands or any of that stuff.

Not that I didn't like a guy. In fact, that was the problem. I only had eyes for *one* guy—one utterly gorgeous, totally unattainable guy—Ben Donovan. *Ben!* Heart stopping. Swoon worthy. The one boy every girl at Hartley High School could agree was a complete babe. Oh yeah—he's had about fifteen girlfriends in the last few years—all of them wannabe swimsuit models. And lately he'd been going out with Claudia Stone, one of Hartley's biggest fashion plates. *Sigh!*

I wouldn't have a chance with Ben even if I could dump my extra pounds, I reminded myself. Ben hung out with Hartley's in crowd—BMWs, best-dressed honors, the works—and I was definitely not on Hartley High's society A-list.

But some dreams were worth having, and Ben was definitely one of them. Sun-kissed, silky brown hair. Sweet, warm hazel eyes that seemed to look right inside you even if he was only passing you in the hallway between classes. And muscular arms and shoulders that rode confidently on his supersexy, six-foot frame.

But it was more than just his looks. It was, oh, the sound of his voice when he spoke up in AP English. His ability to laugh at himself when he goofed up in bio, which we'd taken last year. The comfortable way he had around people. It was a thousand and one things that I couldn't put a finger on. But it *was*. Like water freezes at thirty-two degrees and dogs like to have their bellies scratched. It was chemistry, nature, whatever you wanted to call it. I was in love with Ben Donovan. And he didn't have clue one that I was so much as breathing.

Enough! I snapped my elbow guards into place. *Once the game starts, these negative thoughts are going to vanish into thin air,* I assured myself. That was the great thing about lacrosse. When I was playing, it was as if I was in another world. Not to brag, but I was really good at it too. At most games, as a matter of fact. So you would think I would have gone out for more teams, right? Unfortunately, disaster lurked everywhere—even when you had talent.

When I was eleven years old, I went out for girls' Little League softball. During a big game I stole home and split my pants sliding in. I mean *really* split my pants. And within about five minutes everyone had forgotten about the slide part. All they could talk about was the girl who was so fat, her pants split. Which should have been the end of my sports career, except that lacrosse was my dad's sport in college. It would have broken his heart if I'd quit this team too.

Serena reappeared and shoved a lacrosse stick into my hand. "Let's kick some butt!"

I laughed and faked a scoop, facing the mirror and all. Everything would have been fine then, except at that moment Hartley's cheerleading squad came bounding in.

"Coach Burke is loaning us to you jockettes for your big game," Tami Hess, the head cheerleader, announced, sounding less than thrilled. She whipped off her sundress and began wriggling into her micromini cheerleading outfit. Something so small, it would barely get past my ankle.

"Rah. Rah," I muttered under my breath, feeling my newly found self-confidence seeping into the tiled floor.

"Forget 'em," Serena whispered into my ear. "We're the stars of today's show."

I nodded, turning my back on the cheerleaders' excited chatter. All the talk was about our upcoming junior-class trip. A seriously cool event and something I was actually looking forward to—three days of sports and outdoorsy stuff up in the mountains. No parents and no older sister home from college to get on my case. *Yes!*

"I heard two years ago Josh Clarke had to streak through the campsite on a dare!" one of the cheerleaders said, her voice a stage whisper.

My head whipped around. *Gulp!* I'd conveniently forgotten about *that* part of the trip. On Saturday night the tradition was that those with enough guts would sneak off for some "unofficial" activities. Truth or dare was first. Okay, not so bad, right? Then came spin the bottle—a game I'd sworn off for life.

Ready for another blast from my unhappy past? *It's the sixth grade, and I'm at Johnny Kerr's big make-out party. We're all giggling, girls and boys, and I spin the bottle, which lands on Johnny. I sit up on my knees, all ready for the first nonrelative kiss of my life. But then Johnny starts making this noise. For a minute I think he's sick, dying even, until the other kids start laughing and I realize he's oinking.* The joke was on me.

I didn't go to any make-out parties after that, which was how I ended up being the dateless, never-been-kissed wonder I was now. So no *way* was I playing spin the bottle—in fact, Russian roulette might have been preferable—unless through some miracle I could be guaranteed a kiss with Ben. *Yeah, right!* Ben's girlfriend, Claudia, was one of the best-looking girls in school. The chances he would be playing STB on the junior-class trip were about a billion to one.

"—and then Claudia slapped his face," Tami squealed.

"Get out!" Lucy, the squad's second in command, cried. "I heard she was a complete wreck. Sobbing and—"

"No," Mandy, a third cheerleader, interjected. "It was Ben who was upset because she said—"

"What?" I blurted out, flung back to the present at the mention of Ben's name.

"Didn't you hear?" Tami asked, her big, blue eyes wide with astonishment. "Ben and Claudia are splitsville."

"And that means," the cheerleaders practically gushed in unison, "he's wide open for snagging!"

They were too busy jumping up and down over their own potential chances to pay me any mind. Which was a good thing because my heart was doing serious somersaults in my chest. And I knew one look at my burning face would have spilled the beans on my secret crush. Ben Donovan was *free!* I started to tingle from the roots of my auburn hair to the tips of my toes.

But as I looked around at the competition, their slim, perfect bodies slipping effortlessly into their size-five cheerleading outfits, and then glanced down at my own chubby body, stuffed into my dumpy uniform, I had to ask: *Who am I kidding?* In my wildest dreams how could I possibly stand a chance with Ben against these girls?

Ben

"Hey, Donovan!" I heard a voice yell from down below. "Where the hell have you been?"

Bummer! I suppressed a sigh as my friend Kurt Weston made his way up the wooden bleachers to where I was sitting. Usually I would welcome his company. Kurt was my best bud, after all. But today I'd purposely picked a spot none of my crew would venture to. I wanted to be alone for once.

He tugged on the knees of his khakis to keep the crease crisp and took a seat next to me. "I looked all over the school. What are you doing— hiding out? I hope you're not sulking over Claudia and Chet. You said you were going to dump her."

I started to reply, but as usual Kurt's mouth continued to run. "Girls' lacrosse?" He lowered his voice so none of the few dozen people around us would hear him. "What a loser game." He looked out at the field. "Oh, I see. Checking out the cheerleaders, huh?" He gave me a big grin, and the light glinted off his perfectly capped teeth, a present from his old man on his sixteenth birthday, along with a cherry red Mercedes SUV. In my crowd no one's exactly hurting in the money department.

Kurt ran a large hand through his dark brown curls and then adjusted his Ray-Ban sunglasses. "Hunting for new prospects," he mused. "That's my man, Ben. Tami's really cute." Kurt pointed to the bouncy blonde doing a split. "But that new girl Roxanne is a knockout."

I let my eyes dutifully drift to the brunette cheerleader, but my thoughts were elsewhere. The truth was, I hadn't been looking at anyone. I'd mostly been staring into space, trying to get a handle on my feelings about breaking up with Claudia.

Historywise, I'd been thinking about ending it with her pretty much from day one. But something was always coming up. The annual bonfire. The spring dance. And then all the double dates with Kurt and his girlfriend, Tanya March. It also didn't help that my father thought Claudia was "just perfect." They had barely exchanged two words, but her parents were members of the same country club as my father and stepmother. To my dad's mind, there was no better endorsement than that.

Finally, after going out for two *long* months, I had dropped the ax today at lunch. Lots of sobbing, lots of hysterics. But it all felt kind of hollow. Like Claudia's tears had less to do with losing *me* and more to do with losing the status of *us* as a cool couple. Within minutes she was drying her eyes and flirting with Chet Landsdow, the captain of the tennis team. What was that about?

A sharp elbow in the side reminded me that Kurt was still sitting there. "So come on, Ben. Which one are you going to pick? Tanya's laying odds on Maggie Schiff. I'm backing Tami. But wow, that Roxanne *is* hot."

I shook my head. "You both lose because I'm taking a much needed break." I glanced up at the scoreboard. Hartley was tied with Lincoln, two all, with only a few minutes to go.

"What?" Kurt frowned. "Oh, I get it—you really are singed over Claudia and Chet. Man, you could get her back like this." He snapped his fingers. "You want me to tell Tanya to pass the word?"

This time I couldn't suppress my sigh. "I don't want Claudia back. I'm happy for her. I'm glad she found somebody else. Now I don't have to feel guilty about it."

"That's good," Kurt said, exaggeratedly wiping invisible sweat from his brow. "I thought you were going soft on me. It's not like Ben Donovan to pine over some girl."

"Well, maybe that's the problem."

"Huh?" Kurt looked at me blankly.

"What I mean is," I started, searching carefully for the words, "Claudia wasn't exactly doing it for me."

Now Kurt really looked vacant. "Do you need your head examined? Next to Tanya, she's the hottest-looking thing at Hartley High. That silky black hair? Those huge green eyes? Maybe you'd better make an appointment with your optometrist."

I sucked in my breath and tried again. "There's nothing wrong with my eyes. I can see she's a major babe. It's just after a while, that wears off. I want something more. I want someone I can talk to. Someone I can—"

"Now, *that's* a honey!" Kurt bellowed, pointing to a slender blond cheerleader doing a complicated series of back flips. "She's got Ben Donovan babe-to-be written all over her."

My mouth closed like a trapdoor. It was obvious Kurt hadn't followed a thing I'd said. *Just as well,* I thought. *I'm not sure what I'm getting at myself.*

I'd been in and out of relationships since the seventh grade. I couldn't even remember most of the girls' names. Sure, if I closed my eyes, I could conjure up an endless parade of smiling, mag-cover-worthy faces. But I couldn't recall a single meaningful conversation with any of them.

Whoa! Suddenly the north side of the lacrosse field seemed to come alive. A girl with a shock of long, wavy, auburn hair had the ball and was weaving nimbly downfield.

She was carrying a few more pounds than normal, but despite that, she was incredibly fast. The spectators sitting around us jumped to their feet. "Go, Megs!" someone in the crowd shouted.

"Hey, I know her," I blurted out, leaping up as well. "That's Megan," I told Kurt. "Megan . . . what's her name." I could hardly believe the chubby, quiet girl from my English class could be so graceful on the lacrosse field.

Kurt reluctantly stood also, now that the rest of the bystanders had blocked his line of sight to the cheerleaders. "Jeez, did she just fake out that de-fenseman?"

"Yeah," I cried, stepping up onto my seat to get

12

a better view. "Look at her go." I gave the scoreboard a quick glance. Only a few seconds left. I watched in admiration as Megan swerved around a blocking mass from the other team, passed the ball, and then retrieved it from a teammate on the other side. From about fifteen feet outside the crease, she fired the ball toward the net. *Goal!*

Her teammates let out an ecstatic whoop and quickly surrounded her, chanting, "We're number one!" The crowd in the bleachers took up the cry as well.

"Cool," I enthused. "That girl Megan just pulled down the championship for Hartley High."

"Yeah." Kurt started to clean his sunglasses. "That carrottop was pretty good. Some serious moves. Too bad she's not a hottie."

TWO

Megan

"**H**ey, Mom!" I shouted as I flung open the screen door to our house. "Cyclones rule!"

My mother came rushing out of the kitchen, flour from her latest baking adventure smeared across her nose. Mom freelanced as a cookbook editor, and her first line of defense was making sure the recipes worked. "That's great, honey. It's wonderful you're . . . getting so much exercise."

"Thanks, Mom," I said sarcastically. "I'm sure the Lincoln Lions will sleep better tonight knowing I managed to burn some cals at their expense."

I ran upstairs to my bedroom. Mom tried, but she didn't get it at all. To her, lacrosse was nothing more than a potential weight-loss method. Luckily I'd stopped in at my dad's hardware store in town on

14

the way home and given him a play-by-play. Just to show you how different they were, Dad's first reaction was to clear a space in the window of his store. That was where he would be putting my trophy.

Dad had all my trophies and plaques up in his shop—even though, other than lacrosse, they were all from my Little League days. Today, when he started dropping not-so-subtle hints about my going out for soccer in the fall, I kiddingly told him I wouldn't—for his own good. Any more winning teams and he wouldn't have room to display the power tools.

I dropped my backpack on the floor and rooted through my dresser drawer for my bathing suit. In the last few days the late May weather had turned from warm to hot, and I was looking forward to a victory dip in our pool. Normally I wouldn't be caught dead in a bathing suit, but family was . . . well, family. They were used to seeing Orca the whale paddling around in our private ocean.

I was whistling the Cyclones' fight song when I stepped out onto the patio. Big mistake. My sister, Leah, and her friends must have slipped in while I was changing. I did a quick about-face just as Ross—Leah's stuck-up, Adonis of a boyfriend—did one of his obnoxious cannonballs, flooding my sister and her girlfriends. Luckily the commotion supplied the cover I needed to slip back into the house unseen.

Unfortunately, my trying-too-hard-to-be-helpful mom was hot on my heels. "Megan, where are you going, honey? Leah doesn't care if you swim with her and her friends."

"Maybe she doesn't," I muttered under my breath, taking the steps up to my room two at a time, "but I do." I wouldn't be caught dead in a bathing suit in front of a bunch of college guys.

"You don't have anything to be ashamed of," my mother went on, running after me. "Plenty of girls your age are still carrying some baby fat."

"Gee, thanks, Mom," I said, turning on the landing to glare at her. "Now I'm not only fat, but a baby too?"

My mother gave me one of her consoling-type looks. "You know that's not what I meant. You've got a perfectly adorable figure. Plenty of girls your age—"

"Mom, please, could you just leave it?" I could feel a few tears stirring behind my eyelids. Being confronted about my weight and all the issues it brought up made me crazy.

My mother backed off, and I was able to collapse unmolested onto my dark blue chenille bedspread. Not for long, though. Two minutes later Leah was tapping at my door. "Let me in," she demanded.

I pulled myself off the bed and unlocked the door, easily imagining my mother's whispered instructions: "Your sister's feeling self-conscious about her weight. Try to convince her to come down." Our mom was as predictable as a Nick at Nite rerun.

Leah stood there with a scowl on her face, in her

16

tiny red-and-white-checkered bikini, arms crossed over her totally flat stomach. We were practically mirror images—in the distorted fun-house sense. Same long, auburn hair, same large, light brown eyes, same discreet sprinkling of freckles across our upturned noses.

We were even both exactly five-foot-seven, which was mostly due to our long legs. But when I looked at her, I saw myself slimmed down to a beauty. And when she looked at me, I was sure she imagined herself blown up by a bicycle pump.

Leah pushed past me. *Oh, sure,* I thought sarcastically. *Come right in.* My sister and I weren't exactly what you would call close. Even though I'd been looking forward to her coming home from college for the summer, lately I wasn't sure why. Two words couldn't pass between us without it turning into a major fight.

"Mom says you're being a big, sulky baby up here and I'm supposed to convince you to come down." Nice. Leah wasn't even pretending it was her idea to get me.

"Wow, thanks for your touching concern, sis." I snorted. "*And* for rubbing in the 'big' part."

Leah threw up her hands and started back for the doorway but hesitated at the threshold. She turned and studied me. "This whole fat thing is getting *très* tired. Nobody cares what you look like."

"That's great," I cried, angrily lobbing a pillow at her. Now I really was close to tears. Not only was I fat, but nobody cared. I didn't even matter.

17

Leah slammed my door, and I fell into a total funk. *What am I supposed to do now?* I asked myself. *Hey, I know. I'll completely demoralize myself by reading Miss Pine's comments on my English paper. Good one, Megan.* That should kill any remaining good vibes about today's win over Lincoln.

Actually, I had more than a little curiosity about the paper—B or no. Where had I gone wrong?

I pulled my knapsack up onto the bed and dumped it out. Pens, pencils, notebooks, my calculator and calculus book created a messy pile. I pulled the term paper from between two notebooks and smoothed down a bent edge. The incriminating B stared up at me from the paper's once hopeful purple cover.

"Here we go," I mumbled, and flipped it open. But as I started to scan the page, I realized this wasn't my writing at all. I'd done my paper on George Orwell's novel *1984*. This paper was all about Orwell's earlier novel, *Animal Farm*.

I turned back to the inside-cover page, and that was when I felt an electrical jolt shoot through my body. *Oh my God! It's . . . it can't be . . . but it is!* Ben Donovan's paper! I must have grabbed the wrong one after class today.

I jumped to my feet and began to do an Irish jig around my room, leaping up and down on my bed and practically bouncing off the walls.

Okay, so I'm not so cool. But Ben Donovan's paper! His phone number had been tattooed on my brain since the eighth grade, and now I finally had a real excuse to call him!

18

I only stopped dancing because I was afraid my mother or Leah would burst in, thinking I was having a fit. No way did I want to explain to either of them the godsend that had just fallen into my lap. Knowing my mother, she would want to send me for coaching lessons on how to talk to a boy on the phone. And Leah would just smirk.

Hold on! How *would* I talk to Ben? What was I going to say? I thought about calling Serena and Laurie, but that would lead to at least a week's analysis. And by then another girl would probably have already snapped him up. Timing was critical. I would just have to wing it.

I hugged my knees to my chest, giggling slightly out of nervousness. My goofy, shaped-like-a-football telephone—a present from my dad—never looked so menacing. But I knew I'd better not wait much longer, or I would never have the guts. Already the ugly thoughts were lining up against me: *Ben won't want to hear from you—you're a tubster, you're gross, you're invisible to boys.* I snatched up the phone and punched in Ben's number, praying that my vocal cords would actually work.

Ben

I could hear the shouting before I even started up the stone path in front of our house. *"Zoe Donovan!"* It sounded like a declaration of war. "Show yourself this instant, young lady! We were

19

supposed to be at the club forty-five minutes ago!"

I opened the heavy wooden door a crack, hoping to slip in unnoticed. Wishful thinking! My father and stepmother, Eve, were blocking the entranceway, their faces molten with anger.

Eve's high-heeled sandal was doing a furious rat-a-tat-tat on the tiled foyer floor; a few silvery blond wisps of her usually immaculate French twist lay plastered across her sweaty forehead. My father, his ascot slightly askew, was pacing back and forth, hands shoved in the pockets of his blue blazer—probably as a precaution against ringing my little sister's neck. At ten years old, Zoe was a pro at driving my father and stepmother bonkers.

"Ben," my father barked, pulling me into the house. "Do something! Your sister is really in trouble. The Smithers are expecting her to swim with little Constance this afternoon. How is it going to look if we show up at the club without her? Dr. Smithers is on the steering committee. He and his wife . . ."

I let my eyes wander as my father ranted. I knew Zoe was hiding someplace close by. I could imagine her impish smile, one small hand clamped across her mouth to keep from giggling. The last thing my little sister cared about was the social register.

"Dad," I said, attempting to broker some peace. "Why don't you and Eve head out? I'll try to find Zoe and—"

"Talk some sense into her," Eve snapped. "At this rate she's going to be a complete social pariah by the age of eleven."

My father nodded, patting down his wavy, gray-flecked hair. "Just like Helen. She doesn't know enough to want to be accepted by decent society."

I bristled and hoped Zoe hadn't heard that.

"Sorry, son," my father quickly apologized. "But this is exactly how it started with your mother. First she refused to go to the garden parties, then the country club, and then she started doing who knows what with those huge slabs of metal."

I gritted my teeth. I'd explained to him a hundred times that Mom was creating metal sculptures. Good ones too. She'd already had her work in a few galleries, and a small museum was planning to include two of her pieces in its winter show. Not that it mattered to Dad. To him, anything that didn't involve making a ton of money or meeting the so-called right people was a waste of time.

My mother's decision three years ago to divorce my father and give up wealth, standing in the community, and a coveted spot at our exclusive club was still totally mystifying to my dad. Especially since it was just . . . to be herself.

I shifted my backpack on my shoulder. I guess I had mixed feelings. *Mom did leave us,* I reminded myself. *She broke up the family.* Okay, so a conventional life was stifling for her. But couldn't she have put up with it for our sake? On the other hand, I also remembered the terrible fights she and Dad used to have. Now, in truth, everyone was better off.

My father had a new wife who was totally club

acceptable. Mom was happy, living in an arts community in upstate New York with a very unconventional guy named Dan. Zoe and I spent every summer and school holiday with her.

Sometimes I wished I could be more like my mother—and not care about what other people thought. But that would just lead to more family fireworks—my dad going ballistic every five seconds. So I toed the party line—my father's line—and stuck to hanging with the other kids whose parents were members of the country club. A perfectly non-rocking-the-boat existence.

As soon as my father and Eve were gone—surprise, surprise—Zoe came skipping out of her hiding place in the pantry closet. A grin a mile long plastered across her face.

"Ben, call me," she teased, twisting a messy lock of her long, white blond hair around her finger. "You're so dreamy. We all just love you! *Not!*" She ran down the hallway toward my father's study.

I gave chase, but by the time I reached the room, she was standing behind my father's desk, holding the answering machine hostage. I could see the little red light blinking furiously. "One more step, buster, and these love messages are history," she threatened.

"Don't be rash, Zoe. I'm sure we can work something out." I dropped my backpack to keep both hands free.

She carefully put the answering machine down and angled her skinny body toward the door. Too late. As a hundred-yard-dash champ, I beat her to the entrance and gave her a good tickling. She collapsed at my feet in laughter, screaming, "Uncle."

"Now scram, squirt," I said good-naturedly, giving her a hand up. As much as I adored my little sister, she could be a real pain in the butt.

I leaned back in my father's chair and pressed the play button. Zoe was right. A half a dozen giggling girls had left messages. The big topic: my breakup with Claudia. I was about to hit erase and dump the whole batch when another tone of voice caught my ear.

"Um . . . hello, Ben? This is Megan. Megan Kennedy." *Hey! The lacrosse girl!* Had she seen me at the game? I listened carefully. "I'm in your AP English class? Um . . . I ended up with your term paper, and I was hoping . . . um . . . you had mine? Okay, bye. Oh . . . my number is 555-1313."

Her message was a little shy, but kind of sweet at the same time. I retrieved my backpack from the floor, and sure enough, this wasn't my work. Not with an A-plus! We must have used the same purple cover. If I'd bothered to look at the paper after class today, that grade would have been a major tip-off that I had the wrong one.

I thumbed through a few pages to see what an A-plus report was like and quickly found myself engrossed, so much so that I turned back to the first page and read the paper through from the beginning. Megan had brought Orwell's theories alive with humor and insight. Who would have known she was so smart?

I thought back to the quiet redhead who sat two rows in front of me in Miss Pine's class. She had barely opened her mouth the whole term. I felt kind of sheepish. I was always offering my opinion even when I hadn't finished the books we'd been assigned. *Oh no!* I thought. *She's probably reading my paper too.* Seeing how smart Megan was, I hoped she didn't think I was a total idiot.

I had just picked up the phone to call her when Kurt and Tanya burst into the room. Zoe must have seen them coming up the walk and let them in because I hadn't heard the doorbell chime. I dropped the phone in the cradle.

"Out of the frying pan and into the fire." Kurt laughed. "What hot babe are you calling?"

I shook my head. "Wrong number." Megan would take too much explaining, and I wasn't in the mood to hear myself being mocked or her— after Kurt's comment about Megan's looks at the game—being trashed.

"Aw, come on," Kurt teased. "Give it up. Don't be shy."

"Kurt, leave him alone," Tanya scolded, hopping up on my father's desk and fluttering her dark blue eyes at me. "He doesn't want to tell you. But you can tell me, Ben." She leaned forward so I could whisper in her ear.

I sat back and smiled, my fingers locked behind my head. Let them wonder. *Go ahead,* I thought. *You'll never guess in a million years.*

Three

Megan

"Megs, snap out of it," Serena said, reaching over the sticky cafeteria table to give my arm a good squeeze. "So Ben didn't call you back. Big deal. It's not the end of the world. He probably didn't get the message. Or he was busy and came home too late to call."

"Not so loud." I moaned, although I knew there was little chance of our being overheard in the crowded, noisy Hartley High cafeteria. I'd purposely secured an empty table in the cavernous room's farthest reaches—lunchroom Mongolia; no chance of being seen, let alone eavesdropped on.

I nestled my head back in my arms, its resting place ever since—between choking bites of my tuna-fish wrap—I'd told Serena and Laurie about last night's massive phone failure. And by now half of Hartley High must know what I'd done.

"I'm a total, hopeless idiot," I told them. "Why did I call him? Why didn't I do what any *sane* wallflower would? Return the paper to Miss Pine and let her sort it out." Then Ben wouldn't have even known I was involved. "But noooo," I went on. "I had to take the initiative and try to inject myself into his rarefied world."

Serena's long fingers dug into my arm a little deeper, trying to get me to lift my head. "You had every right to call him about the paper mix-up. You're beating yourself up over nothing. It's not like you confessed your undying love on his answering machine." She let go of my arm and took a sip of her orange juice before pushing her tray aside.

"That's right," Laurie piped up in her high, squeaky voice. "It's not such a big deal. I'm sure by senior year it will all blow over."

"Laurie!" Serena scolded. "That's not the message we're trying to get across here, okay? It was good that Megan called him."

"But I'm just saying that in a few months, maybe a year, no one will—"

"Laurie, in a minute you're going to be wearing that yogurt you're eating!" Serena hissed. "How many times do I have to tell you girls, playing mouse is not the way to get the cheese. We need to bolster our egos, not buy into this whole invisible-girl thing."

I suppressed a giggle. Sometimes it was a total mystery that Serena and Laurie were even friends. They took the exact opposite view about everything. Where Serena was strong and up front, Laurie jumped at her own shadow. But the two of them had been friends since nursery school, and there was a rock-solid bond between them.

"Laurie's right," I muttered. "The Ben Donovans of this world don't go out with girls like us. They don't even acknowledge our existence. I'm a fat blob, and he's a total god. That's all there is to it."

I could feel the heat of Serena's large, chocolate brown eyes boring through the sleeves of my white T-shirt as she tried once more to pry my chin off my arm. "I *know* you're only joking in there. I *know* you're putting on a much bigger act than you really feel. Because you, Megan Kennedy, are one of the sweetest, funniest, coolest, smartest, and best people in this school. And if the Ben Donovans of the world don't see that, then I'm sorry—it's their loss."

I smiled weakly into the crook of my elbow. *Serena loves me,* I thought. But a friend's take on you and a guy's take were two totally different things. Friends—whoever they were—had gotten to know you somehow. They didn't care what you looked like or where you stood on the social scale. But with guys—guys like Ben anyway—outward appearances were everything. And my outward appearance was . . . mammoth!

Serena started to tap her fingernails on the Formica-topped table. "Maybe you're right, Megs.

27

Maybe the Donovans of this world don't acknowl-edge you. But it's about time that they did. Look! There's Ben now, standing by the soda machine. I'm going to go over there and get this whole thing cleared up." I could hear her seat scrape as she jumped to her feet.

My head shot up like a jack-in-the-box. "Don't you dare!" I gasped, my heart pounding a million miles a second. Already I could feel my skin practi-cally breaking out in hives. If Serena so much as blinked in Ben's general direction, I would be out of Hartley's cafeteria so fast, all that would be left was a puff of smoke.

Serena fell back into her seat, laughing. "At least that got your head off the table. Sorry I had to re-sort to terrorist tactics."

"Serena." I shook my head as she wiped tears of glee out of her eyes. "One of these days." I bent down and helped poor, terrified Laurie out from under the table.

My heart was just starting to beat normally when a big smile spread across Serena's face. "Omigod," she said. "Hold on to your seat. You'll never guess who's heading our way."

"Ha ha, Serena," I retorted. "You already got me once today. I'm not turning around."

"No. I'm not kidding. He's making a beeline to-ward us."

I looked across the table at Laurie to share in a little eye rolling. She had the same vantage point as Serena. She would know that little trickster was pulling my leg . . . again. But Laurie's light blue eyes were as wide as saucers, and she seemed frozen in her seat. Unless she'd suddenly turned into the grande dame of actresses, that meant . . .

I whipped my head around and came face-to-face with Ben Donovan.

Ben

Hmmm, I thought, *maybe crashing Megan and her friends' table during lunch wasn't such a great idea.* Three pairs of eyes were staring up at me like I'd just dropped down from another planet. *Obviously I'm interrupting.* I shifted awkwardly on my feet.

"Um, Megan," I said, breaking the ice with all the subtlety of a stick of TNT. "Sorry I didn't call you back last night. I . . . uh . . . got tied up." I didn't feel like mentioning my family squabbles. After my dad and Eve got home, there'd been another shouting match about Zoe being AWOL from the club. I had to play peacekeeper all night long.

Serena, a pretty girl I'd seen around school, broke into a huge grin—like this was the funniest thing she'd heard all day. Megan started as if she'd been kicked under the table. Only the blue-eyed girl remained mute—more like frozen, actually. Like maybe she was paralyzed. Or just really shy, I realized, as her pale skin heated up to a burning shade of red.

I turned my eyes back to Megan. "Double kudos on your big win yesterday. Both you guys." I nodded toward Serena. "You made some clutch moves to nail that final goal."

Megan's face immediately lit up, and I was struck by the way her light brown eyes sparkled. "Thanks," she said. "We really played hard."

"*You* really played hard," Serena corrected her. She turned to me. "Without Megan we'd probably be languishing in last place."

Megan began to blush and smile at the same time, brightening her eyes even more. They were almost golden.

"I've got your paper in my locker," I told her as the bell rang. "Is this a good time to swap back? I can't believe I snagged the wrong one."

"No," Megan protested, grabbing her backpack. "I think I took yours first. I was in a hurry to get to the game. Sorry about that." Megan waved to her friends as we headed out of the cafeteria.

"Well," I joked as we wove our way through the crowded hallways toward my locker. "In the future you'll just have to call me so we can coordinate cover colors. I don't want to end up with your next paper. It's too demoralizing."

She looked at me oddly.

"See, I have a confession to make," I said as we headed down the hall. Suddenly a couple of guys came barreling past us, and Megan and I both had to jump back to avoid getting creamed. Late May and everyone at Hartley had a case of spring fever.

"Confession?" she asked after we managed to find each other in the crowd.

"Yeah. I read your paper."

Megan froze in midstep, almost causing a pileup. She crinkled her nose. "Was it okay?" she asked tentatively.

"Are you kidding?" I grabbed her arm to keep her moving. "It was brilliant. Pine gave you an A-plus."

"A-*plus?*" she asked, her eyes widening.

I nodded.

"Yes!" she said, pumping her fist like Tiger Woods after a twenty-foot putt. "I was worried I'd blown it or something. When I saw that B . . ." Her hand flew up to her mouth. "I'm sorry . . . I . . ."

"It's okay." I laughed. "I'm amazed I did that well." I stopped. "Here we are. Chez Donovan," I said, motioning to my locker.

She fumbled in her backpack and handed me my paper, looking a bit apologetic.

"It's not your fault," I told her. "I haven't exactly been hitting the books lately. Other things in my life have been sort of . . .well, getting in the way." I banged the metal door beside the combination lock—nailing the sweet spot just right—and popped it open. I routed through my stack of notebooks for her paper.

"Yeah," Megan said sympathetically. "I guess breaking up can really be hard. Oops!" She winced. "Sorry, that's the second dumb thing I've said in the last thirty seconds." She was blushing sweetly.

31

"I mean, I heard that you and Claudia broke up, if that's what you're talking about," she added quickly.

"That's okay," I told her. "Busting up with somebody in the cafeteria kind of makes your life an open book, I guess. But you're right—that hasn't helped my concentration level."

Megan nodded. "Even if it is the right thing to do, I imagine there's still going to be a lot of guilt and a feeling of loss."

I held out her paper, staring at her. She didn't even know me, but she'd hit the nail right on the head about Claudia . . . and my mother. She'd spoken about actual feelings. None of my friends did that. I felt myself wanting to talk to her more.

"Hey, it's our man, Ben!" Kurt's muscular arm leaped out of the crowd and hooked around my neck, pulling me into the middle of our group of friends—Tanya, Kevin, Maggie, and Gary. I hadn't even seen them coming.

"Yo, guys. What's up?" I said. Over the top of Tanya's dark brown head I could see Megan had been edged out of the circle. I watched her turn and disappear into the crowd. *Too bad,* I thought. *I didn't even get to say "see you later."* Kurt and everyone obviously hadn't realized she was with me, so they didn't know how rude they'd been. Why would they? Megan didn't exactly run in my circle.

And to tell the truth, I was kind of glad that she'd left. I'd been dangerously close to spilling my guts to a total stranger. One who was firmly in the to-be-ignored-at-all-costs category, at least in my friends' minds. Kurt and the rest of them would have thought I was certifiable. But another part of me wished I'd had a few more seconds with Megan. It would have been nice to put down the happy mask, even if it was with someone who wasn't considered cool.

Kurt pulled me away from the rest of the group. For a second I thought he was going to say something about Megan. But that was only my paranoia.

"Good news, man. Have I got a girl for you. We're talking babe extraordinaire!"

I leaned back against the bank of lockers and let the breath flow noisily from my lips. "You've got to be kidding. I'm finally free. Let me enjoy myself for a few weeks."

"No, no, no, no!" He tapped me on the chest. "This is not your run-of-the-mill cheerleader. We're talking *beauty queen* here. For real. First runner-up in the local pageant." His hands traced a woman's curves in the air.

I suppressed a groan. "Kurt, please. I've had eight girlfriends in the last six months. Five of which you or Tanya fixed me up with. I haven't been single for more than two days this whole year. Not to put down your choices, but I would like, for once, to see if there's anybody I actually want to go out with, instead of just going out with somebody for the sake of it."

Kurt punched me lightly on the shoulder. "Don't be an idiot. I'm going to say two words to you: Alyssa Beaumont." He held up his hands like he'd just performed a magic trick. "Remember? The girl every guy dreams about. This is the first time she's been free since, like, the third grade. The fact that she would even agree to date you is a total miracle. Her last four boyfriends were college guys. So give me a break. Enough with the Garbo act. Tanya's got it all arranged. Saturday night. Jordan's big bash. The four of us hanging at his party. You'll be thanking me later."

He winked, and I got that sinking feeling in my stomach. *Here we go again.*

Four

Megan

Icould barely lift my eyes to the blackboard as I
sat in Miss Pine's last-period class—knowing
that Ben was only two desks behind me, one row to
the right. Ever since that humiliating episode at his
locker two periods ago, all I'd wanted to do was
crawl home and hide under the covers.

On top of the humiliation, I was feeling pretty
angry. Ignoring me was one thing, but Ben's "big-
stuff" friends had practically swatted me aside like I
was some kind of bug. One of those annoying flies
that crashed the party because the screen door was
left open a second too long.

I looked down at my notebook and realized I'd
scribbled black lines all over the page. I took a deep
breath and tried to calm myself. The problem was, it
was more than just Ben and his friends that I was

angry at. I was mad at myself too. I'd allowed it to happen. I'd slunk off like I didn't have a right to be there.

Serena would never have taken that kind of ice-out treatment. She would have asserted herself. But who was I kidding? Ben's posse wouldn't want to hang out with *that fat girl*. I probably got off light with just a snub.

Lost in these dismal thoughts, I wasn't really following the class discussion until Miss Pine called on Ben. Suddenly my ears seemed razor sharp. Could I be hearing right? Was he actually saying what I thought he was?

I twisted my head around to gape at him.

"So, no, I don't have much to say about Jane Austen," he continued, shrugging his broad shoulders before brushing back a strand of his thick brown hair. "She's a chick's romance writer. I don't know how a guy could get into her stuff."

My hand shot up, almost of its own volition.

"Megan!" Miss Pine exclaimed. "I was hoping we would hear from you on this topic since I know Jane Austen is your favorite writer."

I could hear movement around me as my classmates shifted in their seats to stare. Even Ben looked over, giving me a kind of half smile.

Omigod! I couldn't believe what I'd just gotten myself into. Sure, I was doing a little wound licking over the locker incident, and sure, what Ben said about Jane Austen had put my nose out of joint. But to actually say something about it, call attention to myself? *Am I insane?*

36

I felt like I was floating above the classroom. All eyes were on my earthbound body, but I was light-years away, looking down from my safe perch near the ceiling.

I watched with everyone else as the red-haired girl—who never opened her mouth—tossed back her head and stared at Ben. "Jane Austen's writing is celebrated worldwide for its irony and wit. She's recognized as one of the all-time greatest writers of English literature. Her topics may be love and romance, but she's a first-class satirist. If you missed that, it's either because you've never actually read Jane Austen or, worse, you were only skimming pages. It's an unworthy opinion, as Jane Austen might have said. It not only puts down her incredibly insightful and brilliantly witty commentary, but yourself as well."

You could have heard a pin drop in the classroom. I silently applauded my terrestrial body from my seat on the ceiling. Beaming at the proud look Miss Pine was giving me. But suddenly I felt a change of temperature in the room. *Uh-oh!* The other girls were rolling their eyes.

Lucy Walker leaned her head toward her friend Sarah Burns and whispered, just loud enough for me to hear, "That's one less contestant in the Ben Donovan sweepstakes."

"As if." Sarah snorted. "Ben wouldn't give Miss Chubette a second glance!"

With no warning, I was crashing back to earth—my face in flames. What had I been thinking?

Whatever minuscule chance I had with Ben was now utterly out the window—and it was all my fault. The chubette had opened her mouth and blown everything. I bit down hard on my lip, praying the bell would ring—the only thing that could save me—before the hot tears I could feel welling up began to spill.

Ben

"So in this scene where Mr. Darcy refuses to dance with Elizabeth Bennet," Miss Pine was saying, "Jane Austen is writing about more than a snub; she's exploring a clash of social standing and culture. . . ."

I could feel my cheeks burning as Pine continued to lead the class. *Megan skewered you but good, Benny boy.* Talk about looking like a total doofus. That was me all over.

I guess I could have felt really steamed at her. I know some of my friends would have dedicated the rest of their high-school years to making hers miserable. But then, my crowd didn't take AP classes, and I knew that everything she'd said to me, I deserved.

I shifted in my seat to try to take a peek at her, but her long, red hair was hiding her face. I jotted down the pages Pine wanted us to read and leaned back in my chair.

Thinking about it, when *had* I ever read one of

Austen's novels? Never. I was just shooting off my mouth again. Only this time, instead of all the girls nodding and smiling, one of them had actually called me on it. It was pretty gutsy.

Maybe that's the problem with Claudia and those other girls in my group, I thought. *They hang on my every word, whether I have something halfway smart to say or not.* Did they think my ego was so fragile, it had to be constantly massaged? Or did they really have no opinions of their own? Either way, it was boring, with a capital *B.* I could almost feel my brain wasting away when I hung out with them.

As a kid, I loved to read, and my mom and I were always talking about books. But when was the last time I cracked open a cover, except to skim the pages when some paper was due? Literature wasn't exactly a hot topic with the girls I dated. I glanced toward Megan again, hoping to catch her eye.

Brrringgg! Class over. Twenty people shot to their feet. I grabbed my books and stuffed them into my backpack. I wanted to reach Megan before she left. Surely even my petrified brain could come up with one or two intelligent things to say. Hopefully I could redeem myself. At least I wanted her to know there were no hard feelings.

But when I reached the doorway to scan the bobbing, weaving heads in the hallway, I couldn't find a single redhead among them. Megan was gone.

Kurt came loping up the corridor. "Ben, my man, through with the daily grind?"

I nodded and fell into step with him on our way toward the lockers. "What a class. I got my butt seriously burned."

"No kidding?" Kurt said. "I hope you gave as good as you got."

I sighed. "Not really. I made this stupid crack about Jane Austen, and Meg—" I bit my tongue. I didn't know word for word what Kurt would say if I mentioned Megan, but I did know it wouldn't be nice. "—This girl laced into me."

Kurt twisted the tumbler on his locker and popped open the door. "What else is old," he grunted, throwing in his books. "Chicks are always standing up for each other. This Austen babe, is she hot?"

I suppressed a laugh as I opened my locker. "She might be, except she's been dead close to two hundred years." I dumped in my English and math notebooks.

"Gross, necrobabe. What about the one who nailed you in class? She's still breathing, right? Is she sweet?" Kurt slammed his locker shut.

I frowned. "What's that got to do with anything?"

"Excuse me?" Kurt said, pushing my locker door to one side so he could give me the fully raised eyebrow treatment. "If she's not a babe, why are we having this conversation?" He turned up his hands, palms spread. "If you're not going to date her, who cares what she thinks?"

I do, I realized. Megan was smart and, from what I'd seen so far, really sweet. I didn't want her to think I was some kind of lazy bozo.

"Come on, Donovan." He playfully punched me on the arm. "Stop looking so glum. We'll hit the mall. The gorgeous chicks who hang out there will take your mind off AP English in a snap."

"Yeah, sure," I said, following him toward the parking lot. *I could use some distraction,* I thought. But it wasn't my performance in class that I was thinking about. It was something—or more accurately someone—else. Of course I knew I couldn't tell Kurt what was really on my mind. The main thing that Megan had showed me today—guts—was the one thing I was lacking.

Five

Megan

Even with my bedroom blinds drawn and the bedcovers pulled tightly over my head, it was still too bright. I needed to be way underground. In the deepest, darkest cave, where even when my eyes adjusted to the dark, I wouldn't be able to make out my own hand. I never wanted to see myself again. Surely there was a deserted coal mine somewhere on the outskirts of Hartley. A desolate, forbidding place that no one else would ever venture into, so I could spend the rest of my utterly and totally destroyed life—alone!

Loser! Loser! Loser! marched through my brain, along with those stinging words *Miss Chubette*.

I heard a soft rap on my door. "Go away, Mom," I cried. "I don't want to talk about it." My mother had been trying to coax me out of my bedroom for the past forty-five minutes. But I was determined to never show my face again. And any more of her it's-normal-to-blah-blah-blah—fill in the blanks—lectures and I would really go nuts.

"It's us," I heard a familiar voice call back. "We had a mall date, remember?"

"Serena?" I pulled the covers from my face and sat up on my bed. I'd totally forgotten.

"None other. Laurie's with me too. So open up."

"Hi," Laurie squeaked.

I dragged my battered ego to the door and turned the lock, ushering in my friends. "Don't look at me in case I rub off on you," I warned. "My life is completely ruined."

Serena smirked and perched on the side of my dresser. "I guessed it was something like that. You ran out of school so fast, I thought you were having a medical emergency."

I sat back down on my bed and hugged a pillow to my chest. "Hmmm. That doesn't sound so bad. If I came down with a terminal illness, I bet my mom wouldn't make me go to school." *Not that it matters,* I thought. *I'm as good as socially dead anyway.*

"What happened?" Laurie asked, dropping into my desk chair.

I hung my head. I could barely muster the strength to tell them how I'd humiliated myself.

"Megs, come on," Serena prompted. "I bet it's not as bad as you think. You and Ben seemed to be really hitting it off as you left the cafeteria. What could have gone so wrong in a matter of hours?"

"Everything," I mumbled. "I was totally dissed by his friends at his locker. They showed up, and it was like I didn't even exist."

Serena crossed her arms. "So you think you're special? That's what they do: slight, snub, ignore . . ."

"Reject, rebuff," Laurie chimed in.

"Cut, ostracize," Serena finished. "It's how they feel important. Look at it this way—it's a start. Yesterday you'd never even exchanged two words with Ben. It might take him and his friends a few days to get used to you."

I buried my face in the pillow I was holding and mumbled, "It gets worse."

"Uh-oh," Laurie said.

Serena pulled the pillow from my face. "How?"

I winced. I could feel a vein start to throb in my forehead as the memory of my antics in Miss Pine's class flashed through my mind. "I attacked him in class. He said something stupid, and I called him on it."

Both Serena and Laurie's mouths dropped open. But where Laurie looked like she would have joined me under the covers, Serena suddenly leaped to her feet. "You go, girlfriend!" she exclaimed. "About time you started showing off those brains."

"Augh." I pulled up my feet and lay facedown on the bed. "You're the only one who thinks so. Laurie understands the type of social suicide I committed. All the girls in my class stared at me like I had two heads. Lucy Walker said I totally blew my

chances with Ben, and her friend Sarah Burns laughed and called me Miss Chubette."

"Oh, please." Serena snorted. "Those two girls are the biggest wanna-bes at Hartley High. Lucy Walker couldn't get a date with Ben if she paid him. And everyone knows Sarah Burns is so uptight about her weight, she wears a girdle. So forget them. What did Ben say?"

I slowly pushed myself back to a seated position. "Nothing."

"What about after class?" Serena asked.

I shrugged. "I didn't stick around to find out."

"So," Serena surmised, "other than what those two creeps said, you have no idea whether you've ruined yourself or not. For all you know, Ben could have loved the challenge. I bet he's pining away for you right now." She held the pillow she'd taken from me out in front of her. "Oh, Megan, your brilliant mind and supreme lacrosse prowess have driven me mad. I must have you!" She cradled the pillow in her arms, attacking it with kisses.

"Oh, brother," I cried, grabbing for the pillow. "Laurie, do something!"

But Laurie was laughing as hard as Serena. Despite myself, the giggles started to escape from me too. Within seconds we were all having fits.

"What's going on in here!" Leah barked. She and my mother were staring at us from the doorway.

"Nothing," I choked out before dissolving into another batch of giggles.

Leah rolled her eyes. "I see Countess Dracula's made a full recovery. But could you keep it down? You're giving me a major headache." She turned on her heels and stalked toward her room.

My mother shrugged. "She's in one of her moods."

"Like, in, Ross hasn't called?" I said.

"I heard that," Leah shouted from down the hall. "He's visiting his grandmother. He'll be calling any second."

My mother lowered her voice to a whisper. "Do you think you girls could take Leah with you to the mall? I think it would be good for her if she could take her mind off . . . you know . . . the phone."

"Forget it!" Leah hollered again. "I wouldn't be caught dead in public with them."

"Looks like no," I said. Not that I had any intention of going to the mall anyway. Even if Serena was right and Ben didn't totally hate my guts. Who wanted to chance it?

"But *you* are going, right?" my mother asked, looking at me with her big, pleading brown eyes. Eyes that said, if she could get one of her sulking daughters to go out, then life would be that much more "normal."

"Of course, Mrs. Kennedy," Serena smoothly cut in. "That's why we came over here."

"But . . . ," I started.

"Good," my mother said, letting out a big sigh of relief. "I know you'll have a wonderful time. And pick me up a bag of those spicy walnuts from the specialty shop before you come home. I've almost run out, and this newest recipe calls for two dozen."

I strangled a groan. How'd I get roped into this one?

I was peacefully munching on a slice of pepperoni-and-onion pizza with Serena and Laurie on the balcony of the food court when, out of the corner of my eye, I caught sight of none other than Ross Mathers, Leah's MIA boyfriend. *Uh-oh!*

"Is that who I think it is?" I asked, dropping my slice and pointing to the guy below us on the main floor. "Is that Ross?"

Laurie put on her glasses and peered in the direction I'd indicated. "Looks like it. Tall, black curly hair, next to the elevator bank?"

"What's he doing here?" Serena asked, leaning over the railing to get a better look. "And who's that girl?"

I shook my head. Clearly not my sister. That girl was at least three inches shorter than Leah and had a blond bob. My mind immediately jumped to the worst-case scenario. "That snake," I muttered. "What am I going to tell Leah?"

"It might be innocent," Laurie offered between sips of her soda. "You don't know. They might not even be together. Maybe they're just two strangers, waiting for the elevator."

Serena made a face and pointed at him with her plastic fork before spearing a french fry. "Look how she's leaning against him. They're obviously together.

So unless that's his grandmother, he totally lied to your sister. You've got to say something." She slipped the fry into her mouth.

"But," Laurie argued. "He might have just left his grandmother. Maybe he's only asking that girl for directions."

I watched as the glass elevator doors opened and Ross and the girl stepped into the empty box. The doors had barely closed before they were wrapped in each other's arms.

"Yeah?" I spat. "What's he asking her now? And how's she going to answer with their lips glued together?" I turned away, suddenly feeling sick. *What an idiot!* Didn't Ross realize the elevator was made of see-through glass? The whole mall was witnessing his betrayal of my sister.

"The sooner you tell her, the better," Serena said, popping another french fry into her mouth.

"Why me!" I covered my face with my hands. "Haven't you ever heard the line, 'Don't kill the messenger'?"

"Of course," Serena said.

"Well, Leah hasn't! She'll murder me!"

"Speaking of not killing the messenger," Serena said, dropping her voice an octave. "Guess who's coming our way."

I spread my fingers slowly to take a peek. Now I really *did* feel sick—big time. Ben and his crew were riding up the escalator to our level. "I knew I never should have left my room." I gasped, grabbing my backpack and hightailing it toward the game room.

"Whatever you two do," I cried, "don't let Ben know I'm here!"

Ben

Hey! Is that Megan? Out of the corner of my eye I'd just seen the back end of an auburn ponytail flying toward the game room.

"Uh, Kurt," I mumbled. "You know what? I forgot . . . I have to do something at home today." I turned and ran through the Hartley Mall's food court before Kurt or any of the other guys could say boo. *This might be my only chance to talk to Megan—alone—and let her know I'm not angry over what happened in class.*

I found her standing near the Doomstar video game, but it didn't look like she was playing. I walked up and leaned against the side of the machine. "Out of quarters?"

The astonishment on Megan's face confirmed my suspicion. She was trying to avoid me. "Ben! I . . . ," she stumbled, her face turning a pretty shade of pink, ". . . was thinking about strategy."

I smiled. "Then you're ready for a game. Since you annihilated me in class, how about a rematch in something I'm good at?"

"Um, okay," she said a little sheepishly. "If you want."

I dropped my backpack on the floor, plugged two quarters into the machine, and offered her the

HydraMaster character. The three-headed beast couldn't be killed unless you cut off the center head. "I think I better warn you, though . . . those initials there"—I tapped on the screen at the eighth-place spot—"BRD? That's me."

Megan smiled. "I guess I'll have to work really hard, then."

Hold on a sec! Was it my imagination, or was there mischief in the upturned corners of Megan's mouth? *Nah. Must be a trick of the light.* I took the Medusa controls and hit the start button, expecting the game to last only a minute or two. I knew I would totally crush her, so I decided to take it easy—let her accumulate a few points.

The game started, and Megan's HydraMaster began gathering up energy pods from the first room on level one. I grabbed a couple of pods myself, as well as two of the light swords that were concealed behind the stone wall in the heat chamber. Before I could go after her, though, Megan's HydraMaster hyperlinked to level two, racking up double bonus points. *Lucky! She must have accidentally tripped into the wormhole!* It had taken me four weeks to discover that little trick.

Since only one character could hyperlink between any two levels, I had to take the ramp. *Uh-oh!* The HydraMaster was waiting around the first blind curve. I took a slice at one of its heads with the light sword I was carrying, but I got the wrong one. Two new heads popped up in its place! *More dumb luck!* Now Megan's energy level was doubled too.

Unless I could get into the knowledge chamber, there was no way I would be able to take down the HydraMaster. I hit the cloaking button, thinking it would let me dance right past her. *Hang on!* She was spraying me with decloaking solution—*that* was only available on level three. *How'd she do that?* I tried to make a break for it, but under Megan's lightning-fast manipulation, the HydraMaster seemed to be everywhere at once. In an instant she sank her fangs into my Medusa—dining on the snakes that writhed from my head.

"Game over!" the machine boomed. "HydraMaster rules!"

Megan turned to me, laughter dancing in her golden brown eyes. "I thought you said you knew how to play this game."

"You set me up!" I protested, my face beet red. I looked like a total macho idiot now. I'd expected Megan to be like the other girls I'd played against—who giggled and pushed the wrong buttons and spent more time bumping me with their hips than actually looking at the screen.

"Rematch," I cried from between gritted teeth. "I was being gentlemanly."

"Oh, I see." She widened her eyes and smiled sweetly. "You *let* me win. I guess we *should* have a rematch, then. We'll even switch sides. I'll be Medusa."

I nodded, gripping the joystick. *Perfect,* I thought. Being HydraMaster was my forte. *And this time, no more Mr. Nice Guy.* I dropped another couple of quarters in the slot, and we squared off. Within about three minutes I had Megan's Medusa pinned against the wall of the energy chamber on level three. I was firing shot after shot into the beast's belly. *There! I've got her!* I kept firing away, waiting for the machine to announce my triumphant victory. *Hold on!* Why wasn't the machine acknowledging my win?

I glanced up. *Oh no!* Medusa was somehow transforming my laser-pulse volleys into her own energy. The more I fired away, the stronger she was getting. Suddenly the snakes on Medusa's head took flight, landing on the HydraMaster like locusts from a biblical plague.

"Say bye-bye," I heard Megan mutter to herself, seconds before she sliced HydraMaster's head loose from its moorings.

"Game over! Medusa rules!" the mechanical voice sounded again. This game had turned into a clone of my first humiliating defeat.

"How did you do that?" I gasped, staring incredulously at the machine. "I'm total dog meat."

Megan grinned. "You had me going there on the second level. But after I took the cave-dweller's potion, you should have used the antimatter constraints instead of trying to keep me pinned with laser volleys. It's risky, but it's the only way to drain Medusa's power."

"What cave-dweller's potion?" I demanded. No wonder my surefire laser technique hadn't worked.

Megan giggled. "Just a little secret I discovered.

Next time you're on level two, check out the black-ice pool in the antechamber. It's dangerous but worth it." She flipped her ponytail casually behind her. "I don't usually bother when I'm playing for fun, only when I'm trying to beat my high score."

"Beat your high score?" I narrowed my eyes and looked back at the list of high scorers on the screen. The first five spots were dominated by . . . "You're MGK!"

Megan hid her laughter behind her hand. "Sorry. I guess you're going to have to come up with something else to beat me at."

I shook my head and grinned despite myself. Megan was really something. Smart *and* fun to be with. *Hey!* All of a sudden I had a great idea.

"Are you going to Jordan's party Saturday night?" I asked her.

Megan's eyes dropped to her hands. I could see her reverting to the shy girl I'd overlooked all these years. "I wasn't exactly invited," she mumbled.

"Big deal." I shrugged. "You know these bashes. You start out asking twenty people, and pretty soon the whole school shows up. Jordan's place has plenty of room."

She didn't say anything but continued to stare at her fingers.

"Look, if it's about wheels," I said, "I can give you a lift."

"Really?" She looked up, and for the second time that day I saw how pretty she really was. Her face had that classical bone structure—high cheekbones,

53

rounded lips—even if she was a little on the pudgy side.

"Sure. Eight o'clock sound good?"

Megan nodded happily. Suddenly, over her shoulder, I spied Kurt and the guys heading toward the game room. *Donovan, you idiot,* I thought. *What did you just get yourself into?* I'd completely forgotten about my promise to let Kurt and Tanya set me up with the human Barbie doll, Alyssa Beaumont. *Now I have two dates for Saturday night!* Kurt was going to kill me!

"Megan, just remembered, big family pow-wow," I blurted out. "I've got to split!" I grabbed my backpack and dashed out one of the side doors. I didn't stop running until I was halfway home.

My family must have been busy reloading when I was approaching the house because I didn't hear any heavy artillery as I walked up the path. But as soon as I opened the front door, it was obvious World War III was in full swing.

Zoe came running up to me, tears streaming down her face, and leaped into my arms. My back-pack went flying—books, notebooks, and pens spilling every which way. Zoe could barely speak be-tween choking sobs. "Eve . . . (sniffle) wants me to . . . (gasp, choke) take ballet lessons. (Snuffle, snuffle.) I want to keep playing softball (waaaaa . . .)."

I had lowered Zoe to the floor and was patting her back, trying to calm her down, when Eve marched into the foyer.

"Stop coddling the child," she scolded, her gold bracelets jangling as she wagged her finger. "It's ridiculous that she was ever even allowed to play that grubby little game."

"That's not fair, Eve," I argued. "Zoe loves to play softball. She and our mom spent hours perfecting Zoe's throw."

Eve waved her hand in the air as if she were shooing away a gnat. "Please. What has softball ever done for anyone? Ballet is crucial for a young lady to learn poise and elegance. Look at me." She executed an exaggerated pirouette, her long, black skirt tangling between her knees. "Ten years of instruction and I can illuminate any room with my grace."

"You walk like a duck!" Zoe cried. "I'll never take those stupid lessons! I won't!"

Eve's lightly powdered face turned a hideous color of purple. "Up to your room, young lady! This instant!" She clapped, glaring at Zoe. "Bertram!" she hollered for my father.

My father strode into the foyer, his half-rimmed reading glasses and today's copy of *The Wall Street Journal* in his hand. "Yes, darling?"

"Your daughter!" Eve pinched the bridge of her nose between her eyes, signaling in her usual way that she could go on no longer. My father helped her into the living room.

I was gathering up my books and papers from the floor of the foyer when my father returned.

"Son," he said sternly, "we need your help on this. Your stepmother has been more than patient, but Zoe won't listen to her. I know she listens to you. So it's critical that you explain to her the importance of social obligations."

"But Dad," I said, stuffing the last notebook into my backpack and getting to my feet. "Ballet's not a social obligation. She's just a kid. There's no harm in her playing softball."

He shook his head. "All these things are tied together, son. Zoe's forming friendships with kids that we would rather she didn't associate with. There are a lot of very nice girls at the club. Your stepmother and I don't see why she can't play with them—you always did. You never gave us any trouble with your choice of friends. So, please, have a few words with your sister. Try to get her to follow your example."

Some example, I thought as I trudged up the stairs. I now realized it wasn't only Kurt and the gang who were going to have my head on Saturday night. If my father or Eve had even the slightest inkling that I'd just invited status-zero Megan Kennedy to the hottest party of the year, I'd be the one getting the lecture on socially acceptable behavior—not Zoe!

Six

Megan

"**W**e're number one! We're number one! We're number one!" my lacrosse teammates rumbled in a low whisper as we sat together in the auditorium. In a few minutes Principal Winfrey was going to start the school assembly.

Along with the usual school business we were about to receive our division-championship trophies. A small, silver-plated statue for each girl—plus a huge, gold-plated bowl that would soon take its place in the glass trophy case near the main entrance.

I was as psyched as the rest of my teammates, but something else had my temperature rising even more. Ben. And our Saturday-night plans.

When I woke up this morning, I was sure it had all been a delicious dream. But then I noticed my open diary. A quick scan of what I'd written last night proved it was true. I had a *date* with Ben Donovan!

Principal Winfrey walked onto the stage, and Serena gripped my arm. "I'm so excited!"

"Me too," I gushed back.

Principal Winfrey cleared his throat, causing the high-pitched feedback that seemed to start every Hartley assembly. Everyone giggled or yowled, all of us clutching our ears. He tapped the microphone twice and signaled to Mr. Morris, the AV instructor, that he was ready.

"Ladies and gentlemen," Principal Winfrey announced. "We at Hartley High have a proud tradition. . . ."

I leaned back in the padded seat and let my mind wander back to Ben. The idea of going to Jordan's party with him was exquisite and terrifying at the same time. Even with my diary as proof that yesterday afternoon *had* really happened. That he actually played video games with me *and* asked me out. I had to keep pinching myself for fear I hadn't really woken up at all but had been reading my diary—and was sitting here right now—as part of a long, elaborate dream.

Serena leaned over to me, knocking my elbow off our shared armrest, and let out an exaggerated yawn. "Yadda, yadda, yadda. Didn't he give this same speech last year?"

I giggled, glad to give some of my nervous energy an outlet.

Serena cocked one eyebrow. "You haven't heard a word he said," she accused me in a playful tone. "Your head's stuffed with Ben thoughts!"

"Shhh," I warned her, scared that one of the girls sitting near us would hear. "I heard Winfrey. New leaders . . . goalkeepers of something or other . . ."

"Gotcha!" She punched me lightly on the arm. "You're quoting Coach!" Before I could argue . . .

"Let's give a hand to the new division I girls' lacrosse champions," Principal Winfrey cried. Serena and I snapped to attention as applause broke out in the auditorium. "Unfortunately," he went on, "the individual trophies for the team members haven't actually arrived yet."

Bummer! I looked down the row at my disappointed teammates.

"However, we do have here the school's permanent trophy, which I'd like to present to the team's captain, Megan Kennedy. Megan, will you please come up and accept the trophy on behalf of your team."

Omigod! I shifted in my seat, frantically turning from Serena to Becky Saunders, our goalie, and back again. "I can't do it," I told them. "Someone else has to go up there." I looked around desperately, but each of my teammates shook her head.

"We never would've won if it wasn't for you, Megs," Diane, one of our midfielders, said, leaning over my chair to pat me encouragingly on the shoulder.

I turned one more time to Serena, my last-best chance. She didn't mind the attention. She could go up.

Serena shook her head, a big smile plastered across her face. "It's your win, Megs."

The girls started to clap and stamp their feet. "Megan! Megan!"

Somehow I got my legs to work and miraculously made it onto the stage without falling flat on my face. I even got my arms to stop trembling long enough to shake Principal Winfrey's hand and hold up the big, gold-plated bowl for everyone to see. *Phew! Get me outta here!*

I held out the trophy so Winfrey could take it back, but instead he stepped toward the microphone again. *What? I'm supposed to stay up here?*

"I'm proud to announce," he started, "that we've got another winner in the audience. Let's give a warm round of applause to Alyssa Beaumont—back at school after being chosen first runner-up in the local beauty pageant!"

Alyssa Beaumont! I thought. *Gag city!* I looked out into the audience. There she was, proudly swishing down the center aisle in a curve-hugging sundress that had every guy's eyes spinning in his head. As she ever so slowly made her way up the stage stairs, I felt my blood begin to boil.

Alyssa Beaumont had been my number-one archenemy since forever. Well, since sixth grade anyway. She was the one who'd blabbed to everyone in our school about Johnny Kerr's spin-the-bottle party and the whole shameful "oink-oink" incident. What happened at the party was bad enough; everyone knowing about it had practically ruined my life.

Oh! A collective gasp went up as Alyssa stumbled on her six-inch platform sandals as she approached the podium. Ninety-nine percent of the boys in the audience instinctively rose to their feet to catch her. (I say ninety-nine percent because Robby Caul was in a leg cast.) *As if!* Besides Principal Winfrey, I was the only person within twenty feet of her. And with the giant trophy still in my arms, there wasn't much I could do. Even if I'd felt like it, which I didn't.

Alyssa turned on her phony, beauty-queen smile and motioned with her hands for the boys to sit down. I couldn't help thinking that the whole thing was a ploy—so she could show the world that she had every tongue-lolling guy in the audience in the palm of her hand.

She paused dramatically in front of the microphone, widening her big, blue eyes and shaking her blond hair out behind her. "Thank you, everybody," she gushed. "It's great to be back at Hartley." *Yuck!* The applause from the male sector of the population was practically deafening.

Principal Winfrey reached over and took the trophy from my arms, gently propelling me toward Alyssa. All of a sudden I felt practically naked. There I was—in a baggy T-shirt and size-fourteen khaki skirt—standing next to the most beautiful girl in the school. Megan. Alyssa. Beached whale.

First runner-up in a beauty pageant. Which one would you choose? If I could have crawled behind the thick blue stage curtain, I would have.

No such luck.

"Before you go," Principal Winfrey announced, "I've got great news for the junior class! Our trip next Friday will now feature a morning of white-water rafting!"

The blood drained from my face so fast, I thought I would faint. While Alyssa jumped up and down, clapping, I tried desperately to get behind the podium and out of sight. Me in a bathing suit in full view of the entire junior class? *No conceivable, possible, in-this-lifetime way!*

Ben

"Donovan. You owe me big time," Kurt said, shifting in his seat next to me as Principal Winfrey droned on about the class trip. "A date with Alyssa Beaumont! Look at her. Look at that thick blond hair, those big baby blues, those luscious cherry red lips. Was I right? Or was I right? Have you ever seen such a honey?"

"I see, I see," I growled. "Quit elbowing me. You're going to break a rib."

Kurt leaned forward to grip the back of the chair in front of him. "A honey and a half! And if you don't blow it, my friend, you may be experiencing those lips Saturday night!"

I didn't have anything to say to that. *Kurt's right. Alyssa is stunning—model perfect, even.* But the fact was, I'd been looking at Megan. And even though she wasn't wearing a svelte size six, blowing kisses, and winking at the audience, she looked kind of cute in her shy, nonflashy way.

Kurt fell back into his seat. "Man, I feel sorry for the heifer next to her. Looks like she wishes she could crawl under a rock and die." He wiped a tear of laughter from his eye.

"Kurt," I growled. "You sound like a major jerk. She's not bad."

"Give me a break! She wouldn't be allowed in the audience of one of Alyssa's beauty contests."

I found myself gripping the armrests so hard, I had shooting pains in my hands. Kurt was really pissing me off. "I've talked to Megan a few times. She's very cool."

Kurt looked heavenward. "I'm sure she's a *barrel* of laughs, no pun intended." He cracked up from his own lame joke. "But really, how can you even notice her with Alyssa on the same planet, let alone when they're barely three feet apart?"

"Easy," I said through gritted teeth. "Sometimes people prefer someone they can talk to over someone to drool over."

Kurt turned and gave me his full attention. "You're serious, aren't you? You talked to the chunky girl a few times and thought that was okay, so you're thinking you want to spend some more time with her. I can see that, I guess. If I really

63

stretch it. But don't get confused." He wagged his finger in front of my face. "Having a porker for a pal is one thing; dating her would be something totally else. Megan Kennedy is not girlfriend material. Alyssa, on the other hand, is the definition of *datable*."

I shook my head, feeling really disgusted. "At least Megan's real. Your beauty queen is almost too beautiful. She's like plastic or something."

Kurt smacked his forehead. "I can't believe I'm hearing this. She looks like she just stepped off the cover of *Elle*, and you're complaining? Get with the program. Check out the tube, the movies, the fashion mags. Your personal taste doesn't matter. This is beauty. And if you want to look hot yourself and make the other guys green wishing they were in your shoes, then that"—he stopped to catch his breath and point at Alyssa—"is the kind of eye candy you need on your arm."

Kurt huddled toward me in a conspiratorial way. "Look, I'm not a total loser. I know where you're coming from. Believe me, sometimes when I'm with Tanya, I want to scream. But I'm one of the best-looking dudes in school, and she's my match. We make sense as a couple. It's what's expected. You can't go shaking up the social order because sometimes you get bored. At this very moment every one of the guys in this auditorium would cut off his right arm for a chance to go out with Alyssa. And I can promise you not one of them is thinking about her." He pointed to Megan, who had slunk behind the podium and looked like she was about to duck.

I sank down into my seat. *Social order. What's expected.* That was the kind of stuff my father was always saying. I sighed. Maybe Kurt was right. Maybe Megan *was* just buddy material. Maybe the novelty of actually *talking* to someone was screwing me up, and after a few more conversations I would start wondering: Why was I with her when everyone else wanted to be with the other girl?

A hundred-plus guys can't be wrong, right? Maybe I owed it to myself to check out Alyssa at Jordan's party. There might be more to her than the smiling stage act.

I felt a twinge of guilt over Megan but quickly reasoned it away. *Hey!* I told myself. *It wasn't like I offered to take her as a* date. I was only giving her a lift to the party as a friend. Once we were there, we would each be on our own.

I popped a couple of Life Savers onto my tongue, but even then I knew it would take more than a mint to get the bad taste out of my mouth.

Seven

Megan

"Will you look at these prices," Laurie complained, studying the tag on a hot pink Versace bikini as we milled around the swimwear department in the Hartley Mall.

"Forget the prices." I snorted. "Look at the sizes!" I held up a teeny scrap of material in iridescent black that wouldn't cover a troll doll.

"Stop griping, you two," Serena scolded, gliding past us, her arms laden with bathing suits. "You've got to get into the spirit of this thing."

"Spirit of what?" I asked despondently. "Now that rafting's been added, I don't even want to go on the class trip."

"But I thought you liked rafting," Laurie said. "Don't you go with your family every summer?"

I sighed. "That's totally different. My family's

used to my looks. I'm talking about not wanting to be the star attraction of the freak show. I can see it now." I cupped my mouth like a circus barker. "Come one, come all, see the human hippo shooting the rapids."

"Pish," Serena said, motioning with her hand as if to wave away my fears. "You'll look gorgeous. So what if you have a little extra meat on your bones; it means more to love."

"Now you sound like my mother," I complained, pulling a slightly less gaudy maillot from the rack.

"Megan, here's a nice suit." Laurie handed me a plain gray one-piece. "The tag says it 'deemphasizes a woman's figure.'"

The material felt scratchy in my hands. *Ick!* Inside the suit was a complex web of plastic stays. "It's like some sort of medieval torture device."

"Give me that," Serena said, snatching it from my hand and tossing it back across the rack. "That's for somebody's old grandma." She rooted through the rest of my picks. "This blue one's pretty. I like the green. Forget this." She held up another corset-like structure before throwing it aside. "And the rest of these are decent. But why don't you try some of the bikinis? Strut yourself, girl."

I gave Serena a "yeah, sure" look and added a few more plain one-piece suits to my pile. "Like all the guys in our class wouldn't run the other way if I came walking out in a two-piece."

"Not all," Serena corrected me. "One of them doesn't care what size you are, remember?"

I felt a smile growing at the edges of my lips at the thought of Ben. "Maybe."

I followed Serena and Laurie to the dressing rooms and got busy trying on suits. *Hmmm.* It wasn't as bad as I would have guessed. One or two even looked okay. *Eeny, meeny, miney, moe.* I picked a dark purple one-piece with a low back.

Since Serena had to try on every bathing suit in the store and Laurie couldn't make up her mind and kept trying on the same three, I stood outside their dressing rooms, playing salesgirl—giving advice and fetching different styles and sizes.

". . . and that's all guys really care about," I heard an approaching voice say. A very familiar voice. *Oh no!* I turned just in time to see Alyssa Beaumont and her entourage of beauty-queen hopefuls come strolling in, ready to try on their own selection of minuscule bathing suits.

I was standing outside Serena's dressing room, a scarlet red microbikini on a bathing-suit hanger in my hand. The other girls kept walking past, but Alyssa suddenly stopped. With a mean glint in her light blue eyes she made an exaggerated show of looking at me, the bikini in my hand, and then me again. "I don't think so." She turned to her friends, shaking her head. "I *really* don't think so."

The rest of the girls cracked up, and I felt my face turning a hot shade of red, angry tears building up behind my eyes.

Alyssa turned back to me. With her voice dripping venom she lightly put a hand on my arm. "You might want to try Big, Bold & Beautiful across the street. I hear they carry up to size twenty-eight."

Alyssa's friends were clutching each other for support, they were laughing so hard. *I'm not going to cry,* I told myself. But tears had edged to the surface of my lids.

At that instant Serena's dressing-room door flew open. Her dark eyes were blazing, and she looked angry enough to spit fire. She'd obviously heard everything. "Get your tired, bony butts out of my friend's face before you all end up sitting out the junior-class trip in body casts."

The girls scattered. Even Alyssa put some speed into her saunter.

I kept my eyes downcast, embarrassed in front of Serena and feeling even more that I wanted to cry. *What's wrong with me?* Why hadn't I stood up for myself? I was just as angry as Serena. More so, since Alyssa's barbs had been pointed my way. *Well, maybe that's the problem,* went a voice inside my head. *You took that from horrible Alyssa Beaumont because part of you believes that being fat means you deserve to be mocked and shamed.* Bingo!

Laurie slipped out of her dressing room, and the three of us stood in a circle, not saying anything for a moment while we all calmed down.

Serena squeezed my arm. "I hope you're not feeling bad about what those losers said. Because that's all they are—losers."

"A little." I shrugged, not willing to admit how much Alyssa's words had stung. "I wish I had the guts to do what you did."

"Me? All I did was beat you to the punch. I have a bigger, faster mouth than you, that's all."

I looked down at my sneaker, tracing half circles on the dressing-room carpet. "I wouldn't have said anything."

"Sure, you would," Serena insisted. "You spaced on who you were for a second. You forgot you were Megan Kennedy, one of the smartest kids in school, the supreme master of the lacrosse field and the Saturday-night date of Ben Donovan. Another minute and you would have trash talked them into next week."

I gave Serena a weak smile. "Maybe, if I'd re-membered all that, I would have said something. Like in a hundred years."

Serena shook her head. "It'll come sooner than that—you'll see. I bet Saturday night will give you a real boost."

I hoped so, because I was getting way tired of being an easy mark for the likes of Alyssa Beaumont and her crew. I was sick of feeling bad every time a skinnier, prettier, more popular girl told me to. Just once I would like to strut myself—no holds barred. And maybe Serena was right; maybe Saturday night, on Ben's arm, would be the perfect time to start.

Ben

"Cool! What about these, Ben?" Jordan asked. We were standing in the cooking section of the party store in the Hartley Mall. Jordan was holding up the most ridiculous-looking apron I'd ever seen. It had a picture of a giant gorilla clutching a beer can, his huge, hairy belly showing under a grubby T-shirt with the caption Party Animal on it.

"Don't even think about it," I said.

"But there's three of them," Jordan pleaded, slipping it over his blue-and-green-striped polo shirt. "You, Kurt, and I could each wear one."

I shook my head. "Get with the program, Jordie. We're here for paper products." I pushed the cart to the next aisle and began to gather up packs of cocktail napkins and plastic cups. Jordan had estimated there would be at least a hundred people at his party, and we needed to be prepared.

Jordan loped after me, luckily without the apron. "I guess you're right. Those aren't exactly Alyssa's style. She probably wouldn't like them."

"*I* don't like them," I said.

"Yeah, but tomorrow night is all about Alyssa." He wiggled his eyebrows up and down, Groucho Marx style. "You dog."

I snatched up another set of plastic cups and tossed them into the cart. Alyssa's name had brought back all my uneasy feelings. *What am I going to do about Megan?*

Since we'd arrived at the mall, I'd been keeping my eye out for her. I knew we had to have a chat. I needed to make sure there wasn't any "misunderstanding" about tomorrow night. The last thing I wanted to do was hurt her. And walking into the party with her thinking we were on a date and everyone else knowing I was there to meet Alyssa had disaster written all over it.

Megan's cool, I told myself. *She'll understand.* But I needed to let her know the deal.

Jordan grabbed a pair of candlesticks from the shelf. "I'm guessing these are more your speed, Romeo." He waved the candles in front of me. "A little candlelight. A little music . . ."

"Give it a rest," I snapped, taking the candles from him and putting them back. "You're worse than Kurt."

Jordan looked hurt. "Man, what's your problem? I'd give up a year of dates for one with Alyssa, and you're acting like it's some kind of chore."

I sighed. "It's not such a big deal. She's just a girl."

Jordan rolled his eyes. "Just a girl. Listen to him. Like Alyssa Beaumonts come along every day. I know guys who would kill to go out with her. I can't believe Kurt decided to set you up with her over me. I know the value of an Alyssa Beaumont."

I let Jordan rant while I consulted the last items on our list—ice, soda, chips, and dip. That meant a drive to the convenience store on Route 22. The chances of Megan being there were slim.

"Look, Jordan," I said, vamping for time. "I forgot something. You pay for this stuff and load up the car, and I'll meet you back there in, say, fifteen minutes."

I flew out of the store before he had a chance to protest and raced through the mall to the game room.

With any luck, Megan would be perfecting her video skills. But a quick look showed I was wrong. Same in the food court. By this time I was keeping my eye out for Serena and the quiet blonde as well. Megan could have been anywhere, or nowhere, in the mall. But other than calling her at home, this was my best chance. I'd have to search floor by floor.

I was riding the up escalator when I finally spied her riding down. "Megan!"

She turned, looking up, and on seeing me broke into the sweetest smile. And even better, she was alone.

I quickly turned and started trotting down the up escalator, much to the other riders' dismay.

"Hey, what are you doing!"

"Watch it, buddy!"

"These young ones have no respect today!"

Megan was at the bottom, laughing, when I reached her. "You can get arrested that way."

I smirked. "I've got an in with mall security."

"That could come in handy." She twisted the package in her hand and then looked up at me expectantly, obviously wondering what I'd been chasing her for.

"Which way are you going?" I asked, suddenly feeling very awkward. I'd thought the excuses would flow easily, but now, on seeing her face, I wasn't exactly sure what I was supposed to say.

She motioned to the specialty-food shop. "My mom wants me to pick up some jalapeño peppers. Every Friday night we eat a different country's cuisine. Tonight it's Mexican."

"Wow. I thought we were the only family that did stuff like that."

"Really?" Megan asked. "You do that on Fridays too?"

I gave a half shrug, half shake of my head. "We used to. Before my mom left. Now all my step-mother ever makes for dinner is reservations."

Megan smiled at me sympathetically. "That's too bad. You should come over to our place some-time. My mom cooks for a living—she's a cook-book editor. Anything you want, she can make."

"Great! Uh, but . . ." My stomach did a nauseat-ing flip-flop. *Good work, Donovan,* I berated myself. I was supposed to be letting Megan down easy, and now I'd just wrangled a dinner invite out of her. Was I losing it or what? "Uh, Megan, about tomor-row night . . ."

She blinked twice and then looked at me. I could tell by the way she hooded her light brown eyes that she was waiting for bad news.

I took a deep breath. The sooner I got it over with, the better for both of us. "Something's come up. . . ."

She nodded and started to look off in the dis-tance. From this angle I could see that her eyes were looking shiny. "Yeah, okay. I understand." She started to turn away.

"No. I'm still picking you up; it's just . . ." *What am I doing?* I thought. She just gave me the out I was looking for. She was letting me off the hook. I could have walked away. "Can we make it at eight-fifteen?" a voice that sounded like mine, but couldn't possibly be, asked. "My little sister has a sleep over in your neighborhood, and I've got to give her a lift." The part about Zoe having a sleep over tomorrow night was true, assuming Eve hadn't grounded her by then.

The expression on Megan's face switched from disappointment back to happiness. Almost making it worth it. Almost. Because Megan, Alyssa, and I were still hurtling toward each other on a collision course. And if I knew my friends, once we all hit, things were going to get real ugly, real fast.

Eight

Megan

"**H**ey, guys, I'm home!" I practically skipped through the house to the kitchen. "Smells great!" I handed my mom her jalapeño peppers and gave her a quick peck on the cheek.

"You're in a good mood," she commented. "How was the awards assembly?"

"Fine," I fudged, omitting the part about being trapped onstage with the heinous Alyssa Beaumont and the dreaded addition of the rafting trip. No need to get my mother started on one of her you're-fine-everything's-fine jags. I scooped a tortilla chip into a large bowl of guacamole.

My mother swatted me with her dish towel. "Not till dinner; you'll ruin your appetite."

I grabbed another handful of tortilla chips and

danced out of the kitchen, inches from the snap of my mother's towel.

Leah was in the living room, sprawled across dad's leather E-Z-Boy, painting her toenails a revolting green. "I see the Amazon's home. Could you keep it down? I'm trying to watch this show."

I flopped on the floral couch and glanced at the TV. A woman was talking about laundry detergent. "It's a commercial."

"Preemptive strike," Leah snarled. "So why don't you run along before you really become annoying?"

I rolled my eyes, but even Leah's "mood" couldn't dampen my high. I *still* had a date with Ben. For a minute there, back at the mall, I'd really thought I was history. The way he was hemming and hawing, I'd thought for sure he was trying to take the invitation back. But he didn't! I grabbed one of the tapestry throw pillows and hugged it to my chest. We were still on, tomorrow night, as planned!

"Megan," Leah warned, "I can feel you over there. You're giving off hypervibes that are definitely messing with my calm. Please leave."

I tossed the pillow aside. *What a killjoy,* I thought. I got up, but only to check out the telephone message pad. Nothing was written on it, but that didn't mean someone—like you know who—hadn't called.

"Any calls for me?" I asked. As soon as the words left my mouth, I knew I'd made a big mistake. Leah gave me *the* nastiest look. She even went so far as to put the nail-polish wand back in its bottle. "You were at the mall with Frick and Frack—who else did you possibly think would call? A boy?"

I'd obviously hit a sore spot. As far as I knew, Leah still hadn't heard from Ross. But she'd just pushed my buttons in a big way. "Yes! A boy! It's not unheard of."

"It is for you," she said, throwing back her head to laugh.

"More like for *you!*" I shot back. "When was the last time Ross called?" It was a low blow, but I couldn't resist. I'd had enough of people putting me down today.

"I could go ten years without hearing from Ross and still have gotten a billion more calls than you'll ever get! The only time a boy ever dialed you was either by mistake or to make an obscene phone call!"

That's it! I thought. Time to take out the heavy artillery. I jumped from the couch. "Oh yeah, well, at least if a boy isn't calling me, it's not because he's playing sucky face with some other girl behind my back at the mall!"

"What!" Now Leah leaped to her feet, sending the bottle of nail polish, emery board, and wad of cotton balls flying. "What are you trying to say?"

"Girls! Girls!" My mother came running into the room, jumping between us. Which was a good thing because we'd squared off across the living-room rug, and in a minute the fur was going to fly. "What's going on in here?" she gasped.

Leah pointed to me with a shaking finger, her

face the color of boiled tomatoes. "Miss Thing is trying to make up tales about Ross and another girl at the mall."

I shook my head. "Sorry, no. I was at the food court with Serena and Laurie. We all saw him. He wasn't with his grandmother the other day; he was with some blonde, and they were . . ." I couldn't say it.

"Are you sure it was Ross?" my mother asked, obviously wishing I would change my story.

"Believe me," I said, softening a little when I saw Leah's face turning from red to white, "it was him."

Leah looked at me, her skin taking on color again, her eyes narrowing to two tiny, angry slits. "Lies. All lies. This is some jealous scheme you and your misfit girlfriends concocted. Really, Megan, I know you're low, but I didn't think you'd sink this far."

"Why should I?" I cried. "Ask him if you don't believe me!"

"Forget it! I wouldn't waste my breath." Leah dropped back down onto the E-Z-Boy, her arms crossed. "This is obviously some pathetic attempt to sabotage my love life because *you're* a complete loser on the dating front."

"Well, that's where you're totally wrong," I shouted. I'd been planning to keep my date with Ben to myself. The last thing I wanted was interference from my sister or mother. But now I was seriously seeing red. "I have a date, and it's for tomorrow night!"

"What?" Both my sister and mother stared at

me, their jaws hovering somewhere around their knees.

"That's right," I said, raising my chin an inch. "His name's Ben Donovan, and he's awesome. He's coming to pick me up at eight-fifteen."

My mother steadied herself on the back of the couch for a moment, and then her fist flew up into the air. "Yes!"

I watched dumbfounded as she started to jump around the room as if she'd just found out we'd won the lottery. I was glad I'd made her happy, but *really!*

"Mom," I started, a queasy feeling rising up in the pit of my stomach. What happened to being *fine* just the way I was? Apparently my previously date-less status was a bigger deal to my mom than she'd been letting on. How was she ever going to look me in the eye if this date with Ben didn't work out? *Worse yet,* I wondered, *how will I ever live with her disappointment?*

Leah grabbed the remote to the TV, raising the volume to drown out my mother's glee. "I'll believe it when I see it."

Ben

Jordan's Volvo had barely slowed before I leaped from it onto the curb in front of my house. One more second of inane chatter about his party, and what a lucky guy I was being set up with Alyssa, and I was going to scream. *Gimme a break!*

I just wanted to slip quietly into my room, fall into a coma, and wake up three years from now after the whole disastrous party had come and gone.

"Tomorrow night, dude," Jordan shouted from his car window as he pulled onto the road. "Be there or be square."

I gave a despondent half wave as I dragged my feet up the path toward my house. *Face it, Donovan,* I told myself. *You're toast!*

I was halfway to the door when it flew open. Zoe's tight, compact body came hurtling over the threshold, practically knocking me onto the grass. "Hide me!" she cried.

Our stepmother was in hot pursuit, her mouth twisted in anger. Her long, bloodred talons reached for Zoe's arm. "Hold her!" Eve screeched.

"What's going on?" I demanded, shielding Zoe behind my body without letting her go.

Eve stamped her high-heeled foot on the ground, leaving a stiletto mark in the dirt. "I'm late for the club," she screamed. "Zoe had better be in my Audi in two seconds, or she's grounded for life!"

"I won't! I won't! I don't want to go to ballet!" Zoe wailed, hanging on to my polo shirt, stretching the back as she sank to the ground behind me. "I've got a game to play."

"It's not up to you what you want!" Eve hurled back. "I don't have time for this! Get in that car!"

"Eve, Eve!" I held up my free hand to say

enough. "I'll take Zoe. You go to the club. I'll see she gets to her lesson."

"You can't!" Zoe cried, twisting her arm, trying to break away from my grip. "The team's counting on me."

"Stop!" I snapped at Zoe, pulling her to her feet. "Let Eve go." That seemed to calm my little sister down, or at least she realized it was futile to try to break away from me.

Eve tossed me the keys to my father's BMW. "Make sure they put her in Mr. Alexander's class. He knows how to deal with irksome students." She smoothed down the skirt of her pink Chanel suit and then marched toward her car. She pulled out of the driveway, spraying gravel.

"You've got to take me to the softball game," Zoe pleaded. "The team needs me. Suzy Allen's arm's in a sling. I'm the only one who can pitch."

"C'mon, Zoe," I said, pulling her toward the Beemer. "They'll find someone else. We can't always have what we want." *Isn't that the truth.*

"No, they won't," she cried. "This is really important. I've got to be there."

"Zoe." I sighed, shoving her in through the driver's side so she couldn't make a break for it. "You know Dad and Eve are expecting you to take ballet lessons. Softball is out now." *Just like I'm expected to hook up with Alyssa,* I realized. *So we Donovans had better grin and bear it.*

"I don't care about that. Mom used to let me play. She knew how important it was. I wish Mom

82

were here now." She covered her face with her hands, her thin shoulders jerking under the white material of her T-shirt.

I put a hand on her back, but she pulled away, squeezing into the farthest corner of the passenger seat.

Nice work, Ben, I commended myself sarcastically. Zoe and I'd always been as thick as thieves, and now I'd turned myself into one of the enemy. What was the matter with me? I looked down at my sweet little sister, who wanted nothing more in the world than to play on her softball team, and felt like my heart was being squeezed through a vise. I was trying to drag her—worse, pressure her—into taking ballet lessons I knew she hated. What kind of conformist jerk was I? The worst kind because I knew how bad that felt.

"Zoe," I tried, but her sobs only got louder. I started the car and backed out into the street. At the intersection I tried to reach her once more. "Which way?"

She didn't answer but kept her face buried in her arms. "You're going to be way late if you don't tell me, squirt. Right for Hartley Field or left for the playground?"

It took a moment before Zoe cautiously raised her head. She gave me a look, not quite trusting what she'd heard. The cars behind us were building up and starting to honk their horns. "The field or the playground?"

"Really?" she asked, a ghost of a smile playing across her lips.

"I think I've been enough of a total creep for one day, don't you?"

Zoe dried her eyes and started to laugh as she pointed to the right. I hit the gas, and we shot off toward the softball field.

Nine

Megan

*W*ill this really work? I wondered, staring in the mirror. *Or am I totally hopeless?*

My date with Ben was only an hour away, and Serena, Laurie, and my mother were buzzing around my seat in front of Leah's vanity table. My mother was busily perfecting a French braid, and my long, auburn hair was being brushed, pulled, and twisted in all directions. Serena was applying blush and powder to my cheeks, and Laurie was displaying a stash of Leah's lipsticks for my inspection.

Even Leah was helping—sort of—from her position on the bed. She was stretched out in studied nonchalance, providing the kind of *constructive criticism* that older sisters excel at. "Too much blush. Pull out a few wisps of hair from her braid. Don't use the orange-based lipstick; it'll clash with her coloring." She flicked another page of her magazine. "Not that I believe any of this date business, mind you."

I nodded knowingly as Serena whispered, "Sour grapes!" in my ear. Leah still hadn't talked to Ross, but I wasn't about to bring *that* up.

I grinned at the pretty girl who was smiling back at me from the mirror. The taupe eye shadow had brought out the green flecks in my eyes, and the rose-colored lipstick had given my teeth a toothpaste-commercial brightness. *It really is working,* I realized. *I've never looked this good.*

We all piled back into my room, and I started to fling clothes onto the bed. Everyone agreed I should wear something dressier than my usual jeans or khakis. But despite what my mom said about wearing a dress, I didn't want to be too formal. I was on the fence over a pair of black capri pants and a snug, sleeveless, black cotton top with a scooped neck.

"It's fabulous," Serena cried. "Trust me. Ben's going to love it."

I stepped in front of the full-length mirror. I did look pretty hot—except it was obvious I wasn't a skinny minnie. No way was I going to step through the front door of Jordan's party showing so much of my "bigger" body.

"I can't, Serena," I said. I was nervous enough about the date. I couldn't go . . . exposed. I'd have to wear a baggy top.

"Try this."

I turned to see Leah standing in the doorway.

She tossed me an olive green shirt—one of her favorites. "It's sheer enough so you won't lose the effect, but it will add just that bit of cover to make you feel comfortable."

I grinned at my sister. "Thanks."

Leah rolled her eyes. "You'd better show Dad. He and Mom are already late for their movie, but he didn't want to leave without seeing the finished product."

I ran downstairs. My father stood up as I walked into the living room. He smiled at me, and there were tears in his eyes. I stopped short. *Tears?* I would have expected those from Mom, but my dad too? Was he also over the moon because I had a date, like somehow that made me a better person?

My father reached out and gave me a big hug. "My little girl," he whispered in my ear, "soon she'll be off to college."

I started to laugh. He didn't care about the date part. He was just having his goofy dad feelings. Same as when I lost my first tooth and hit my first home run in softball. It was the growing-up part that was making him misty-eyed. *Men!*

Ben

"I'm warning you, Zoe, no funny stuff," I said, pulling up outside Megan's. I turned to my little sister with my sternest look. "Megan is a friend, so keep your tricks to yourself."

Zoe giggled as she scrambled into the backseat

of our dad's Beemer. *Please be good,* I thought, cringing at the diabolical plans my pip-squeak of a sister might be concocting. Zoe was notorious for torturing my dates. She'd done it all—from sneaking under the dining-room table and tying one girl's shoelaces together to dropping her pet mouse in another one's lap. I hoped Megan was tough enough for a mischievous ten-year-old.

As soon as I rang the Kennedys' front bell, the door swung open. *Whoa!* I felt my jaw start to drop and quickly righted it into a smile as Megan stepped onto the porch. I could sense from the giggles that there was a group of girls standing in the hallway, but I didn't notice any of them. I only had eyes for Megan. She looked fantastic.

Her hair was pulled off her face in one of those fancy braids, and her clear, rosy skin glowed. She was wearing sleek black pants, a black sleeveless top, and a flimsy olive shirt that gave a tantalizing glimpse of skin rather than the tight, in-your-face look that some of the girls in my crowd preferred.

We were halfway to the car when my little sister's impish face popped out of the window. I felt my stomach give a lurch. *Zoe!* I'd forgotten all about her. I ran around to the passenger side of the car and opened the door for Megan. The light from the streetlamp showed me that Zoe had poured a thin layer of talc on the black leather seat. I quickly wiped it off. "That better be all of it," I whispered furiously to Zoe. I stepped back so Megan could get in.

But Megan stopped at the door. She took one

look at Zoe and jerked back her head. "Oh no!" she cried. "Not you!"

My heart jumped. "What, Megan? Has she done something to you?" I felt sick. Was Zoe branching out and torturing girls that I wasn't even dating?

"She sure did," Megan said, wagging her finger at Zoe. "This little she-devil totally trounced our team last week. We couldn't get one hit off her the whole game!"

Zoe's face broke into a grin that could have lit up Hartley in a blackout. "You're the Kennedy's Hardware coach."

"That's right." Megan nodded. "Ben, you didn't tell me your sister is the L&T She-Devils' ace pitcher. Whole teams cry when she takes the field!"

Now it was my turn to grin. "You'd better cut it out, Megan; Zoe's head's going to get so big, it'll pop."

Megan laughed and started to get into the car, but Zoe leaped out of the backseat.

"Wait!" she cried, grabbing Megan's arm. "I might have, um, left something on the seat . . . by accident."

Sure enough, after I'd wiped away the talc, Zoe had secretly spilled a thin puddle of water. She quickly wiped it away and for good measure laid her sweatshirt across the seat. "You can't be too careful," Zoe said innocently.

I smiled to myself. Now, that was a first. Megan had totally won over my incorrigible kid sister.

After we dropped Zoe off at her girlfriend's house, I started heading toward Jordan's. I kept sneaking glances at Megan. I couldn't believe how great she looked. Just as beautiful as the girls I was used to hanging out with. But would my friends think the same? *Not a chance.* They were so caught up with the whole 'zine concept of beauty, they would never be able to look beyond Megan's extra pounds.

I slowed the car practically to a crawl as we reached Jordan's gated community. It was the last place I wanted to go, but did I have a choice? Maybe. I kept my eyes on the road as I took the plunge. "I was thinking, Megan. Maybe we should give the party a skip. . . ."

I glanced over to see how she liked the idea. *Not much.* She was staring back at me, and her lower lip was trembling. "If you don't want to take me . . ."

Whoops! She thinks I don't want to be with her. I stopped the car at the side of the road. "It's not that. It's just . . ."

"I understand. All your friends are going to be there. You don't really want to be hanging out with me." She lowered her eyes and stared down at her hands.

I shook my head. "Not at all. I'm psyched to be with you. It's just . . . it's just . . ."

Megan lifted her eyes to mine, waiting for my reason. But what answer could I give her? That I'd agreed to be set up with this other girl? That even though I thought she looked beautiful, my friends would never see it? *How lame can you get, Donovan?*

"Forget it. Just preparty jitters. We'll have a great time," I assured her. I revved the motor and pulled into Jordan's long, winding driveway.

Ten

Megan

I took a deep breath and followed Ben through the open door into Jordan Kirby's crowded, noisy living room. The room was dark except for strings of novelty lights that had been strewn across the mantelpiece and tacked to the ceiling. Dancing couples shimmied to distorted rap music that blared from the speakers, killing any hope of conversation. I was relieved when Ben nudged my elbow, gently guiding me down the hallway to the kitchen.

"Jordan never knows when enough is enough," Ben grumbled. "We'll get a pop and hang out in the family room. Coke or root beer?" He held up two bottles.

"Root beer," I said, and took it from his hand. I glanced around the kitchen. A group of Ben's friends waved at him from the far corner, near a restaurant-style refrigerator. But other than that, we had the massive room to ourselves. My mother would have wept at the size of this kitchen. The preparation area was nearly as big as our living room, and it had every modern convenience, including a huge, professional six-burner stove.

"My mom would think she'd died and gone to heaven in here," I told Ben.

He nodded, looking around. "And I bet Jordan would be thinking the same thing if your mom cooked him a meal. I've tasted Mrs. Kirby's food—yuck."

I was still laughing when Tanya March broke away from the group in the corner and glided up to us. "Ben! There you are. And Marge, is it?"

"Megan," I corrected her.

Tanya waved her hand. *No matter.* The only problem was her hand was holding a full glass of cranberry juice.

I gasped as the cold liquid hit my chest. *Omigod!* Two of the girls from the group in the corner began to laugh.

Ben rushed to the sideboard and grabbed a roll of paper towels. He ran back and handed them to me. "Good going, Tanya," he said sarcastically.

"I'm so sorry," Tanya gushed, practically wrestling the roll from Ben's hands. She ripped off a sheet and started to blot at my arm. "I didn't mean to be such a klutz."

"It's okay," I said. "I can wipe it off." I took the paper towels from her hand and started to work on the front of my shirt.

"This is no good," Tanya complained. "It's going to stain. Come on, we'll rinse it out."

I didn't like that idea at all. That meant taking off my protective covering. Who knew how long I would have to wait for the top to dry? "Really, it's fine, Tanya. Not a problem."

But Tanya wouldn't let up. It was almost as if she wanted me out of the room. "Ben, tell her to let me help her. I feel awful."

Ben shrugged as if to say, *That's girl stuff.*

Tanya put her hands on her slender hips, clothed in a pair of skintight jeans. "You're going to make Ben think I did it on purpose."

I winced. Now she was putting me on the spot.

She broke out into a hundred-watt smile. "C'mon. I won't bite. Any friend of Ben's is automatically a friend of mine." She grabbed my arm and started to tug, leaving me little choice. *Gee,* I thought, *Tanya's never even acknowledged my existence. Is hanging with Ben all I have to do for her to be nice to me?*

In the mauve-tiled guest bathroom Tanya was quick and efficient. I shrugged out of Leah's olive green top, and she gave it a quick soak. I was still worried I'd have to sit out most of the party while I waited for it to dry, but Tanya found Mrs. Kirby's hair dryer under the sink and gave the shirt a good blast. All in all, we couldn't have been away for more than ten minutes.

When we returned to the kitchen, Ben was gone. "He must be in the family room," Tanya said, with a wink. "We'll catch up to him there."

I followed her down a long, carpeted corridor and then up a flight of stairs. "The family room's upstairs?" I asked.

Tanya shook her dark brown hair and motioned with her finger for me to follow. "We'll go up on the balcony. That way we can look down and find him right away."

The balcony overlooked a huge room with a stone fireplace. There was a piano in the corner and two couches facing each other in the middle. About twenty people were milling around, chatting with each other in loose groups. I could still hear the music, but it was much less obnoxious this far away. I spied Ben talking with Kurt and Jordan.

"There he is," I said, and started to walk toward the stairs.

"Wait," Tanya called, laughter in her voice. "Look who's here!"

I turned back. A hush seemed to have come over the downstairs crowd. The French doors leading to the patio stood open, and Alyssa Beaumont was sauntering into the family room. She was all in white—long, flowing dress and high-heeled sandals—and her blond hair hung in loose curls around her shoulders. I could practically hear the collective gasp from the guys who turned to watch her walk. A walk that led directly to Ben.

I watched, rooted to the ground, as her lean, shapely arm reached up and her long fingers possessively adjusted the collar of Ben's blue, button-down shirt. I felt my self-confidence begin to buckle.

At that moment Tanya leaned forward and whispered in my ear, "Aren't they adorable together? When Ben agreed to be set up with Alyssa tonight, I didn't know *what* would happen. All of his friends were hoping they would hit it off. And look, it's love at first sight!"

Tanya skipped off, and I felt the dream I'd been living come crashing to an end. Only instead of waking to reality, I'd been plunged into the worst nightmare ever. *This isn't happening,* I told myself. But it was. It was, and I had to get out of there. I had to get home.

I stumbled toward the staircase, tears blinding my eyes. *Now I know what Ben was trying to tell me on the way over,* I realized. *And at the mall yesterday!* This was no date. It was just a ride. An errand of mercy. And Ben had obviously regretted even offering me the lift from the beginning. But I was so pathetic that I'd made it impossible for him to get out of it. Everyone who saw us together must have been thinking: *Poor Ben, what is he doing with that porker?* Ben was here to meet Alyssa, and I was obviously the laughingstock of the party. The pitiful fat girl who mistakenly thought somebody liked her.

I hid my face as I hurried down the hallway, practically throwing myself out the Kirbys' front door. It was the sixth-grade spin-the-bottle game all over again, only a million times worse. Because this was Ben. The guy I loved more than anything. And it was obvious that he felt nothing for me.

Ben

"Of course, *poise* is the first thing the judges look for," Alyssa said authoritatively. She casually flipped a lock of golden blond hair over her shoulder. "It's not enough just to look great. You've got to carry yourself like a winner. I always try to . . ."

I stifled a yawn and glanced around the ever widening group of males that had surrounded Alyssa and me. A few more minutes of polite chitchat and I would have done my duty. *I promised Kurt I would meet Alyssa, and now I've done it.* So far, so good—no major explosions. But disaster was still a definite possibility. I wanted to find Megan and get out of there.

"But you must know that, Ben," Alyssa said, tugging me by the sleeve.

"Uh, yeah, sure," I said, trying to cover my inattentiveness. The finer points of beauty competitions didn't exactly grab me. Plus I was trying to keep an eye out for Megan.

I looked at Alyssa, and our eyes locked for a moment. She was beautiful, but she seemed to be a carbon copy of the other girls I'd gone out with. All looks and no substance. Dye her hair black and give

96

her green contacts and she could be Claudia.

"Excuse me," I said, extracting myself from the proprietary hand that Alyssa had somehow placed on my shoulder. It was high time I found Megan. As I stepped aside, the other guys—who'd been lapping up Alyssa's beauty-pageant war stories— quickly took my place.

I checked the kitchen first, then the downstairs bathrooms and even the noisy, mobbed living room. No Megan. I took the stairs to the balcony level above the family room for a bird's-eye view. Maybe we'd been missing each other—maybe she'd been in the kitchen while I'd been in the living room, and while I was in the kitchen . . . *oh, brother!*

From the balcony I spied Tanya in the family room, whispering to Alyssa. "Tanya," I shouted, waving until I got her attention.

Tanya waved back and motioned for me to come down. *Finally,* I thought, *she must know where Megan is.* I headed downstairs.

"Ben," Tanya exclaimed, taking my arm and maneuvering me toward Alyssa, who coolly slipped her hand under the crook of my elbow. Kurt was standing nearby, talking to Jordan. "Perfect timing! Alyssa and I were just saying we'd like to go out for pizza at Pepe's. Kurt," she called, "we're ready."

"Sorry, not tonight," I said, liberating myself from their grip as politely as possible. Tanya and Alyssa were obviously trying to hijack me. I could only guess it was because of Megan. "Um, Tanya," I said, pulling her aside. "Where's Megan?"

Tanya nonchalantly examined her nails. "Don't worry about her. She's been gone for ages. We'll just hang like usual and have a great time."

"Are we set?" Kurt asked, joining Tanya and me. "I squared it with Jordan. We'll come back here after the hordes clear out."

I ignored Kurt, still staring at Tanya. "What do you mean, ages ago? Why did she leave?" I didn't like the sound of her flip comments at all.

Tanya gave me one of her Pepsodent smiles. "I think she was afraid of the stroke of midnight. You know, turning into a pumpkin and all."

Kurt started to laugh as Alyssa came up to us. "What's so funny?" she asked innocently.

"Ben lost his friend." Tanya giggled. "Megan Kennedy."

Alyssa gave me a mocking glance. "Ben," she cooed, "I hope you're not trying to make me jealous."

"As if." Kurt snorted.

I ignored Kurt's crack. "Did someone give her a ride?"

Tanya shrugged.

Great, I thought. *This is exactly what I was hoping to avoid.* "I've got to check." I excused myself and hurried toward the hallway, pushing my way through the throngs in the living room. *Maybe I can still catch her.*

But the long gravel driveway was deserted. Not a wisp of red hair in sight. And I couldn't drive after her because my car was boxed in by two others. Megan could be halfway home by now—if not already snug in her bed.

Tanya caught up with me as I stood by my car, surveying the hopelessness of the situation. "Ben," she said softly.

I whipped my head around and glared at her. Even though the whole disaster was really my fault, I couldn't help thinking that Tanya had had a hand in Megan's sudden disappearing act.

"Truce. Okay?"

Obviously I wasn't hiding my anger very well.

Tanya leaned against my car. "Megan left when she saw how perfect you and Alyssa looked together. She didn't want to be in the way. I'm sure there're no hard feelings. She could have stayed. No one told her to leave."

Kurt pulled up in his SUV—apparently he'd had the good sense to park on the side of the house. Alyssa waved from the backseat. "Next stop, Pepe's garbage pie," Kurt called, tooting the horn.

I sighed, kicking at a bit of gravel. Maybe Tanya was right. Maybe she and Kurt—and even Megan—understood the world better than I did. Megan had obviously seen how impossible it would be for us to hang together. By leaving, she was saving us both a lot of trouble and maybe heartache too.

I climbed into the back of Kurt's car, same as every Saturday night. This was where I belonged. I'd been friends with these people since the sixth grade.

Alyssa leaned a little closer to me. "I'm sorry

about Megan ditching you like that," she teased. "I hope I'm not too poor a substitute."

What was I supposed to say? If I insulted Alyssa, it would be like dissing my whole gang. "That's okay," I muttered. "She's just a friend."

"That's nice," Alyssa purred, her hand lighting momentarily on my forearm. "I hope we'll be friends too."

I turned and glanced out the window. *If I see Megan walking along the side of the road, I'll make Kurt stop*, I resolved. Otherwise it looked like another night of going with the flow.

Eleven

Megan

I've never been so glad to see my house, I thought, blinking back tears. The place looked as dark as I felt, and that was fine with me. I'd been praying that my parents were still at the movies and that Leah was out with her friends. If anyone had been home, I would have had to hide out in my childhood tree fort until they'd all gone to bed.

There was no way I would have been able to face my mother, or my sister, tonight. Not that it mattered, but I didn't know what would be worse, Leah's smug I-told-you-sos or my mother's disappointment at what a fat, utter failure I was as a daughter.

I stumbled into the house and pulled myself up the staircase, not even bothering to turn on the lights. I wanted my bed and the feel of the cool covers on my burning face. I wanted to hide from everyone and everything forever.

My only hope was that I was so insignificant to Ben's crowd that the whole disastrous nondate wouldn't even have registered with them—as surely as it hadn't registered with him. By tomorrow morning I would have come up with a story for my mother and Leah, and hopefully, in a month or so, it would all blow over. Though I knew it would take a lot longer than that for my heart to heal.

But as I rushed down the hallway, using my hands to guide myself, Leah popped out of her bedroom. I gave a strangled cry. She must have been sitting in the dark because I hadn't even seen a light under her door.

I tried to push past her, but she grabbed my arm. I closed my eyes, waiting for the snide comment that would push me over the edge and back into teary oblivion. But instead her voice was gentle. "What's wrong? What happened, Megan?"

"Nothing," I started defensively. But then the thought that someone—anyone—was actually being nice to me made the floodgates open again. And the fact that it was Leah, who I would have expected a slap from, made me want to tell her the truth.

I staggered toward the wall, leaning against it for support. I could feel the warm tears flowing down my cheeks. "You were right," I said, my voice hoarse and trembling. "It wasn't a date. He was there to meet another girl."

Leah wrapped her arm around my shoulders and led me into her bedroom. The room was dim, the only light coming from the dull flicker of a candle. There was a box of tissues on her bed, and I could see a few of them wadded up on the floor around her wicker wastebasket. *Leah's been crying too,* I realized.

"Not a good night for the Kennedy girls," Leah said lightly, giving my shoulder a squeeze as we dropped down on her bed. "You were right about Ross." She sighed and fell onto her back.

"What happened?" I asked.

Leah laid her arm across her eyes. "I finally confronted him at the mall tonight." She gave a small laugh. "In the food court. First the little worm tried to get out of it. But when I told him you'd seen him with that girl and he tried to call *you* a liar, I really let him have it. Ketchup all over his brand-new white sweater."

I couldn't believe that after all I'd been through tonight I could be laughing, but the image of Ross covered with ketchup was too much.

"I'm sorry I was such a jerk," Leah went on. "Part of me knew you were telling the truth about Ross. I guess I knew he never really loved me. He never once looked at me the way Ben looked at you tonight when he came to the door. I don't know what happened at your party, but I would kill to have a guy's face light up that way."

I tried to take in her words and find comfort in them. But Leah hadn't seen the way Alyssa had *claimed* Ben. Everything about her seemed to say, *You're mine now.* I blinked hard, trying to wish away the image of Alyssa reaching up to Ben's collar. Even if he had liked the way I looked when he picked me up or even if he thought I was the greatest thing since sliced bread—how could he resist Alyssa now that she'd made it known she liked him?

Aren't they adorable together? I could still hear Tanya's words. And with all of Ben's friends behind it, I knew I was history.

"Thanks, Leah." I sniffled, plucking a Kleenex from the box to wipe my eyes. "But I'm afraid it's a hopeless case." Any chance I'd had with Ben was gone forever.

Ben

"This is one of the most irresponsible stunts you've ever pulled, Ben," my father said, for the *second* time.

"Dad . . . ," I started hopelessly. *Jeez, now I know how Zoe must feel,* I thought. If I'd known this was what I was coming home to, I would have braved another hour of Alyssa's mind-numbing chatter and gone back with the gang to Jordan's party!

My father and Eve stood on either side of the mantelpiece, hovering over my seat on the living-room couch. They were both in their bathrobes, obviously having waited up long past their bedtimes so we could have this "chat."

I hadn't so much as stepped through the front door when my father had started lacing into me. I should have known it would happen eventually, but Mr. Alexander, the ballet school's instructor of *irksome* students, had wasted no time in ratting out Zoe for missing today's lesson.

"And *how* did this happen?" my father demanded. "I'd like to believe that you drove her to ballet but that *she* snuck out the back when you weren't looking. But I know you are far too conscientious about your little sister, Ben. I *know* you would have personally seen her to her classroom. Which leads me to conclude that you never took her there at all."

"And you specifically promised me," Eve chimed in, looking like a cold-cream commercial—her face lathered in blue goo.

"Dad. Eve." I turned from one to the other. "Please. Softball's *really* important to Zoe. She loves playing. And it turns out she's the team's ace pitcher. I think it's really great that—"

"Enough," my father cut me off. "The point isn't what your *ten-year-old* sister wants or even that she skipped ballet practice. The point is that you allowed her to skip it. Your stepmother and I can understand it coming from Zoe."

"That's right," Eve added stiffly, "your father and I know that Zoe's only an uninformed child. She doesn't understand the importance of keeping up appearances and making good impressions . . . yet."

"True, Eve," my father agreed, before turning back to me to continue his speech. "But you, Ben. You should have known better. We're very disappointed in you."

It went on like that for another half hour before they finally released me. As soon as I got into my room, I threw myself down on my bed. I was sick and tired of the whole keeping-up-appearances and making-the-right-impression rap. What about what I wanted? Or who I wanted?

Like Megan? a little voice inside me asked. I tried to ignore it, but it had already bubbled up from my unconscious. *Megan.*

I shook my head, but the image of her sweet, pretty face smiling at me from her front door remained. And no matter how much I tried to tell myself that I'd done the right thing by going off with Kurt and the girls—that she and I could never be—I couldn't get her out of my mind. *I should have gone after her,* I thought. *I should have gone to her house and explained.*

I'd done right by my friends and right by my father's way of thinking, but who was I kidding? I could sugarcoat it any way I wanted—try to convince myself that it was best for Megan, for both of us—but the truth was I'd done totally wrong by her. And maybe even myself. *What a jerk.*

Twelve

Megan

"Megan, what's going on?" Leah shouted. "You've been up here for hours, and you're still not packed. Mom's got the engine running. They won't hold the bus for you. You'll miss your junior-class trip!"

I barely lifted my eyes from my empty duffel bag. It was Friday morning, six days after my Hindenburg disaster of a date with Ben, and I still wasn't even *close* to being over it.

"I'm not going," I said. I gave my sister a woeful look. "I can't. The idea of three days of watching Ben and that horrible Alyssa in some kind of love fest would be too awful for me." A few tears squeezed out of my sore eyes and dripped onto the back of my hand.

Leah pushed aside a pile of my shirts and sat

down on the bed next to me. "Look. Maybe you've got it all wrong. Have you talked to him? What did he say when you called him back?"

I shrugged. "I didn't."

Leah raised an eyebrow. "What do you mean, you *didn't?* I told you he called *days* ago. I wrote down the message."

I grabbed one of my T-shirts and twisted it between my hands. "I got the message loud and clear on Saturday night. I don't need it spelled out for me. 'I'm going out with Alyssa now. . . . Let's be friends . . . only we hardly know each other, so forget that. . . . Let's go back to you being invisible.'"

Leah shook her head. "I doubt he'd say that."

I stood up and started to pace the length of my bedroom. "Close enough. You haven't seen them at school. First you see Ben, then you see Alyssa—like two coats of paint. I saved us both the embarrassment. And I made sure I stayed out of his way."

Leah scooped up the toppled-over pile of shirts and dropped them into my duffel. "Then you can continue your avoidance routine during the weekend trip."

"No," I said, trying to prevent her from adding my jeans to the bag. "That'll be impossible. There's no telling where or when they might pop up."

Leah pulled the duffel bag away from me and tossed in my toiletries. I tried to grab it back from her, but she hung on tight. "Megan," she panted. "Give me this bag!"

"No!" I shouted back.

Finally she let go, and I went flying across the room, tripping over my bed onto the floor, the contents of the duffel bag spilling out on top of me.

"Fine. You win," Leah said in exasperation. "But you can't stay up in your room forever. You can't live your life hiding from other people every time you get your feelings hurt."

"It's more than my feelings," I cried, climbing back onto the bed. "It's my heart."

"Then fight for him," Leah snapped.

I hugged the duffel bag to my chest. "I can't. He won't want me. Not with Alyssa around."

Leah crossed her arms and let out a deep sigh. "You're being silly. This isn't helping anything. The only way to get over a broken heart is to get back out there. Do the things you love. And that means having fun and hanging out with your friends. Serena and Laurie are going to be there, right?"

I nodded.

"And the whole trip's about competing in outdoorsy sporting events?"

I nodded again.

Leah gently extracted the duffel bag from my arms and began to fill it once more. "Megs, this trip's got your name written all over it. Don't throw away this good time because someone else is too blind to see how great you are."

Leah's right, I thought. *I've been looking forward to this trip for ages.* Before my mind got derailed with Ben thoughts, the three days was going to be about having a blast with my two best friends. That was what it could be about again.

The loud blaring of a car horn made us both jump. "Come on," I heard my mother shout from the driveway before leaning on the horn again. "I don't want to have to drive you all the way up to Redwing Mountain!"

"And she will." Leah laughed. "And then she'll volunteer to be a chaperon and she'll want to bunk with you. You know you don't want three days of that!"

"Tell me about it!" I grabbed my duffel bag. Things were bad enough as it was. "Thanks, Leah," I said, before racing down the stairs.

Who knows? With any luck, maybe I wouldn't see Ben or Alyssa for the whole weekend. With any luck at all.

Ben

"Oh, Ben, you're so cute," Alyssa gushed. "I love it when you make that face."

"Really?" I said. The only expression on my face was one of utter boredom. That or outright pain. We were two hours into the trip up to Redwing Mountain, and my butt was getting seriously sore. Though not half as sore as my ears.

Alyssa hadn't shut up once since we'd pulled out of the Hartley High parking lot. She was in the seat directly in front of mine but had popped up and leaned over the back of her seat almost the minute the bus took off. I was sitting next to Kurt, who was pretending to be asleep, thinking he was doing me a favor by giving Alyssa and me "private time."

"I went to a palm reader in New Orleans during the pageant," Alyssa said, holding her hand out in front of me. "She told me all about my love life. Want to know what she said?"

I sighed. Flirting with Alyssa was the last thing I wanted to do. I'd spent the past week at school putting up with my friends' none-too-subtle efforts to push us together. *It's like I've been on a tightrope all week,* I thought. Hanging out with Alyssa enough to keep my friends off my case but not doing anything to push us over the line into being an item. Which had left me with no time to square things with Megan.

I'd been trying to speak with her ever since the mess up at Jordan's party, but she never seemed to be around. I'd haunted the cafeteria during lunch period, lingered outside Miss Pine's classroom— only to find out Megan was doing an independent-study project in the library—and even called her house. But she'd never called me back.

This bus ride seemed like my best chance. I'd jumped out of the front bus as soon as I'd realized Megan would be riding in this one. Here, at least, she couldn't disappear into thin air like she'd been doing at school all week. To improve my chances, I'd deviously stowed my backpack directly above Serena Jefferson's seat, guessing Megan would be joining her. And sure enough, right before the buses pulled out, Megan had hopped breathlessly on board and sat beside her friend.

"See, this is my love line," Alyssa said, slowly tracing a line up the palm of her hand. "Let's see yours."

"Uh, sorry, Alyssa," I said. "I'm not really into all that hocus-pocus stuff. I think I'm going to get my Discman and listen to some tunes." I didn't want to be rude, especially with Kurt keeping an ear on our conversation. But if I didn't try to talk to Megan now, I might not have another chance. I stood up.

Alyssa's fingers circled my arm. "Want company?"

I forced a smile and gently removed her hand. "I think I can manage."

I strolled up toward the front of the bus and casually rested my arm across the back of Megan's seat. Serena was asleep, her head resting against the window. Megan glanced my way.

"Hey," I started to say, but the words caught in my throat. Megan had turned away from my smile. She wasn't even acknowledging me!

I straightened up fast and began fumbling in my bag on the rack above her seat. I yanked out my Discman and quickly rushed to the back of the bus. My cheeks were burning. Anyone with half a brain would have known what had just happened. News flash: Ben Donovan went up to talk to Megan Kennedy and she totally iced him.

Anyone except Alyssa, that was. As soon as I

sank back into my seat beside Kurt, she was up on her knees, hovering over me again.

"What are you listening to?" she exclaimed. "'N Sync?"

"I don't know. Muddy Waters, I think." I'd been getting into some of the old blues stuff my mother's partner, Dan, was always sending me, but I couldn't remember exactly what I'd put in the Discman. All I could see in my mind's eye was the way Megan had turned her head away.

"I love Matty Waters!" Alyssa cried. "She's very cool."

"Him," I corrected her. "*Muddy* Waters is a guy. A blues guy."

"Oh, whoops!" Alyssa giggled. "Caught me. But I'd like to hear him, Ben." She fixed me with a sexy look. "Maybe we could go see him when he comes to town."

I closed my eyes. "He's been dead since '83."

She bit her lip and wrinkled her nose cutely. A stellar performance that I'm sure would have made most of the guys on the bus totally cave and pledge their undying love. But the only scene affecting me was the one that I'd played a starring—and humiliating—role in at the front of the bus a few minutes ago.

"Here," I said, holding out the Discman to her. "Why don't you give him a listen and let me know what you think."

"Oh, I'm sure I'd love him . . . if you do."

I smiled right back at her. "Really, I want you to check him out."

Alyssa looked a bit disconcerted. It was obvious the last thing she wanted to do was listen to some old blues guy she'd never heard of. I almost felt sorry for her. Almost. Except that it would give me an hour of uninterrupted peace!

Alyssa had no sooner put on the Discman earphones than Kurt sat up straight. He leaned toward me, lowering his voice in a conspiratorial whisper. "Tonight. Definitely make the move tonight."

"Huh?" I gave him a blank stare, although I knew he was talking about Alyssa.

He rolled his eyes. "I know you're not that dense, Donovan." He indicated Alyssa's seat with his chin. "She's not going to wait around forever. And there's a line of guys a mile long ready to take your place."

I sighed and glanced out the window over his head. We were off the highway now, and the hills around us were thick with evergreens.

Kurt narrowed his eyes. "Funny you went to collect your Discman and you didn't even know what was in it."

I shrugged, feeling a tightening in my jaw.

"You know what else is funny, now that I think of it?" Kurt went on. "That sudden need of yours to switch to this bus when we were already set up on the other one. And how you left your bag all the way up front."

"I've heard it's bad luck to ride in the front bus of a caravan," I said. "And as far as the backpack goes, why lug it all the way back here?"

114

Kurt scraped his chin with his nail. "Bad luck, huh? I thought you didn't believe in all that hocus-pocus stuff."

"Whatever," I said.

Kurt leaned in even closer. "Look. I know if there was someone other than Alyssa, you'd tell me, right? Like you always have. Unless of course you were too embarrassed because maybe they were sort of . . ." He puffed out his cheeks.

I could feel a dull throbbing sensation building up behind my eyes. Anger. Maybe Megan *had* dissed me. Maybe she would never have anything to do with me again. But I didn't want to hear Kurt start trashing her. Kurt was like the Terminator. Once he got hold of something, he would never let up.

I knew the best way to handle him was to play it cool. I leaned my head back on my seat rest and smiled. "Don't worry, Kurt. I'm not thinking about anybody."

"Good," Kurt said, closing his eyes as Alyssa scrambled on top of her seat again. "All yours."

Thirteen

Megan

"Y ou won't believe what happened," I told Serena, shaking her awake as soon as my heart stopped pounding in my chest. "He came up here!" I didn't need to tell Serena who *he* was. "I thought I was going to have a coronary."

Serena sat up, wiping the sleep from her dark brown eyes. "You're kidding. What did he say?"

I bit my lip. "Nothing. He sort of smiled, but I turned away."

"Megs." She punched me. "Why did you do that?"

"Ouch!" I rubbed my arm. "He wasn't here to talk to me. He got something out of his bag and split."

Serena gave me a big eye roll. "His bag? Like, hello? What was it doing above your seat in the first

116

place? He wanted to talk to you. I still think he has a thing for you."

I shook my head, but before we could discuss it further, the bus erupted into a chorus of, "We're here!"

As we pulled up alongside the leader bus, I eagerly took in the long expanse of lush green grass dotted with log cabins and towering pine trees that made up the Redwing Mountain camp. *Awesome!*

The bus jerked to a stop, and everyone began piling out. The camp staff and school chaperons immediately began barking orders, handing out cabin and sports-team assignments and rushing everyone off.

"The mess tent is closing in five minutes!" a harried camp counselor bellowed. "Drop your bags in your cabins and get back here ASAP!"

I felt like I was in a horde of frightened sheep as I rushed to the side of the bus, where our luggage was being piled on the grass. I snatched up my duffel bag. In the mayhem I'd lost sight of Serena and Laurie, but I wasn't worried. I was sure we would meet up at the cabin.

I hurried down the dirt trail, following the signs to cabin A. I couldn't help smiling at the thick flowering bushes, the inquisitive chipmunks that darted before me on the path, and the glimpses of the meandering river I was catching through the trees. The Redwing Mountain camp was gorgeous. The air was so clean, I could almost taste it.

I staked out a top bunk toward the back of the

cabin, hoping to keep two nearby bunks free for Serena and Laurie. But as my cabin mates began to file in, quickly claiming the beds around me, I realized that there was only one space left. Either Serena or Laurie had obviously been assigned to a different cabin.

Wrong! I realized, with a sick, sinking feeling in my stomach. *I* was the odd man out. The last person to saunter into the cabin wasn't either of my girlfriends. No. It was the very last person I wanted to see. And she would be sleeping right across from me for the next three nights!

"I'm here, girls!" Alyssa called out, as if we'd all been sitting around waiting for her. She wheeled her bag between our bunk beds and gave me a smug smile. "Don't you hate those long drives? Time for a quick change." She bent down and unzipped the suitcase, pulling out a carefully packed, supershort, hot pink halter dress.

"I think I know someone who'll like this dress," she murmured, loud enough for only me to hear. "Don't you?" There was a positively mean glint in her blue eyes.

She tossed the dress onto her bed before slipping out of her trendy, flowered sarong and white cotton top in full view of our cabin mates. She stood there in her fancy lingerie for a full five seconds, as if she were posing for the judges in a swimsuit contest. Finally she stepped into the dress.

I instinctively wrapped my arms around my stomach. The sight of her slender, perfect body made every bad feeling I'd ever had about myself race up and lodge in my throat. I felt inadequate and jealous and roughly the size of a Mack Truck. *Ben won't only like that dress,* I thought. *He'll love it.*

I swallowed hard as tears stung my eyes. Seeing her face-to-face like this reminded me of how easily she'd been able to snare Ben away from me. *And why not?* I thought, turning my face to wipe a tear. All anyone had to do was look at her and then look at me. No contest. I didn't stand a chance.

I pretended to busy myself with my bag, trying to regulate my breathing and keep myself from letting go with an all-out sob. If I could have crawled back onto the bus and returned to Hartley, I would have. My weekend was totally and obviously ruined. With Alyssa as my cabin mate Ben would be around constantly, a continual reminder of my lowly status in the social order—a loveless fat girl that nobody wanted.

Ben

Please let me fall asleep! I mentally begged the slumber gods as I punched my neck buster of a pillow and flopped onto my left side. My bunk bed in cabin D was way too short, and the mattress might as well have been stuffed with bricks, it was so hard. Plus my stomach was rumbling like a freight train from the so-called food we'd been given at the canteen. But those annoyances were nothing compared to the incessant buzz of my fellow cabin mates.

"That Gina Wong is so-oo fine," Stan, one of the guys from the basketball team, was saying.

"Yeah, and her friend Toni isn't half bad either," someone else chimed in. "She's got those long legs. . . ."

Girls. Girls. Girls. They'd been going on like this for what seemed like hours. *Haven't they ever seen females before?* This weekend was going downhill in a hurry. Between Megan totally ignoring me and Alyssa trying to attach herself to my arm like a fungus, my chances of having a decent time on this trip looked like less than zero! I'd hoped for a little peace and quiet at bedtime. But *nooo!*

"Guys, give it a rest," I growled. No one heard me as the topic turned to tomorrow night's spin-the-bottle game.

"Do you think Liza will play?"

"Keep dreaming, Andy. She wouldn't kiss you even if your bottle did land on her."

"I've got my dibs on Evie," Stan called out.

"Too late, Stan the man—Evie's going out with John, but I heard Marsha just broke up with Luke."

"If Marsha plays, I'll be there for sure."

"Augh!" I cried, shooting up in my bunk and practically banging my head on the ceiling. "Enough! I'm sick and tired of hearing about girls. Can't we just have a guys' weekend? Bushwhack some trails into the woods? Hike up to a lake and do some fishing or something?"

The cabin broke out into hisses and derisive

catcalls. "Easy for you to say, Donovan," Stan called out from two bunks over. "With a hot tamale like Alyssa to call your own, it's not like you've got anything to worry about."

"She's yours. Take her!" I screamed.

"Really?" Eight guys sprang up from their bunks and began to babble even more.

"You two aren't sewn up?"

"She's going to play?"

"I've got a chance?"

Then Kurt lumbered to his feet from the bunk under me. "Now, hold up, guys." He raised his hands. "Ben's only joking. Alyssa only has eyes for him."

"Thanks a lot, Donovan," Stan called out. "Rub it in!"

"Yeah, D-man," Andy cried out. "Don't gloat. Nobody likes a poor winner."

"Ohhh!" I groaned, burying my face in my pillow. This was hopeless. *Nobody gets it at all!*

Fourteen

Megan

"Come to Megan," I whispered, lying on my belly beneath one of the gigantic evergreens on the steep precipice that overlooked the dirt path below. My paint gun was pointing downward and ready for action, propped between two low-lying branches. I could hear members of team D—the enemy—approaching along the path.

My team—team A—had done some serious damage, but I knew for a fact there were a few renegades left. One of them maybe even was Ben.

My hand started to shake at the thought of him, but I took a deep breath and willed it steady. I'd been having a blast the whole day, and I didn't want to start falling apart now. Especially since our team had a shot at first place. We'd won the morning's relay races but only taken second in the treasure hunt. A win in the paint-gun wars would put us back on top.

Suddenly there was silence and then the sound of scrambling feet as my prey mounted the easier part of the craggy hillside. I held my breath, hoping that even if they stumbled upon my hiding place, the mud I'd smeared on my face and purple jump-suit and the leaves I'd woven through my hair would keep me camouflaged.

The sound of marching feet kept going, and I sat up. I couldn't see who it was through the thick ground cover, but from the color of their jump-suits—black—I knew it was the enemy. I whistled like a whippoorwill to signal my group that danger was approaching.

Whiff! Whiff! I heard from a distance. The un-mistakable sound of the air guns we'd been issued.

"I'm hit!"

"Ugh," I groaned to myself, "too late." That was my teammate Chiara's voice. This game was getting too close for comfort. Who knew how many of us were actually left? Team D had gotten lucky early in the game and had quickly taken out five of us. And a few—like Alyssa—had surrendered in the first few minutes rather than get all dirty.

I stealthily began creeping through the woods toward the sound of laughter I could hear to my left. *Fools!* I thought. *They're going down for this!*

I crouched on my haunches to reposition my gun. Suddenly two of my teammates, Ryan Andrews and Julia Baron, practically fell over me as they stumbled along the path.

"Shhh." I put my index finger up to my lips and pointed in the direction of the laughter I'd heard. Now there was only a deathly silence. I imagined an ambush waiting to happen.

"You two split up," I whispered. "When I give the signal, Julia, you make a commotion by that fallen tree. Ryan, position yourself behind that rock. I'm going to get down by the riverbank to lie in wait."

Julia and Ryan nodded and quietly tiptoed to their positions. A second later Julia started her ruckus.

"Ow! Help, you guys. I'm stuck. Hey, you guys!" she was calling out as she rustled the nearby bushes.

I darted through the woods toward the enemy, throwing myself over a huge log and then squirreling into a pile of leaves. The sound of their footsteps was getting closer as they cautiously moved in, lured by the noise Julia was making. I leveled my paint gun, squinting down the barrel as I trained the crosshairs on the open space I knew they would traverse—my finger itching on the trigger as my next victim came into sight.

Ben

"I'll handle this, Donovan," Kurt said, motioning for me to stay behind him on the path. "I'm the paint-gun king!"

I rolled my eyes at the back of his black jump-suit. True, he had single-handedly taken out five of team A's players, but he'd also sacrificed three of ours to do it!

"Yes, sir," I joked, and clicked my heels to-gether.

Kurt turned around and gave me a sour look. "Shhh! I can hear them just up ahead."

So can I, I thought. *So can the whole forest!* I didn't like it. I didn't like it one bit. That kind of deliber-ate noise was like Morse code: *t-r-a-p!* "Kurt," I whispered, "let's think about this."

"And lose a golden opportunity? No way." He kept moving toward the noise.

"Really, I'm stuck real bad," the girl's voice echoed around us.

I grabbed his arm. "Seriously. It doesn't sound right. Who'd be dumb enough to make all that noise?"

He gave me his superior I'm-in-charge look. "They're amateurs. Who's left? Ryan, Tom, a cou-ple of girls—your friend Megan? They're not that devious. One of the girls probably tripped over a vine and got her sneaker caught. The rest of them will be trying to help her. This is going to be great. Like shooting fish in a barrel."

I shook my head. Kurt was way underestimating Megan. I hadn't seen her since the paint-gun game started, but I'd heard about the carnage. She'd taken down six of our teammates, and they'd never seen it coming. She was still out there. And I would bet a chest full of paint that she knew we were too.

Kurt turned around to motion me on. "Come on, wuss, I promise you nothing. . . ."

But before Kurt could utter another word, a pile of leaves seemed to rise up in front of us. We both froze until I heard the telltale *pffft* of an air gun. Kurt's black jumpsuit exploded into bright pink.

"Gotcha!" Megan cried, leaves falling from her shoulders like a shower. Her gun swung, pointing straight at me.

I gave a small yelp and tried to ready mine. *Too late!* I had just enough time to see the smile curl on her lips before the yellow paint splashed my chest.

Megan's teammates came crashing through the underbrush, hollering, "Team A rules!" and surrounding her in a frenzy of high fives and back slapping. I couldn't help smiling at what a great time she was having. Even though she was a total mess, mud smeared across her cheeks, her red hair a rat's nest of leaves and twigs, she actually looked pretty cute.

It took a moment, but I finally caught her eye. I grinned, and she smiled back at me. That seemed like a good sign, so I took a step in her direction. But before I could get any farther, Kurt got ahold of my arm, spinning me around. "Come on," he growled. "No fraternizing with the enemy."

"In a minute," I said, pulling away, but as I turned back, Megan had been swallowed up by her jubilant teammates, who were proudly leading her back to their base camp.

"That was the luckiest break I've ever seen," Kurt spat as we made our way back to our base. "She was probably cowering there the whole day. Good thing for her we walked past, or the camp counselors would have found her in the morning, frozen in that spot."

"Admit it, Kurt," I needled him. "She got you but good."

"No way."

Zach Spencer and Randy Eton caught up with us on the other side of the clearing. "Who got you?" Zach asked.

"Some chick," Kurt snarled. "Her gun went off by mistake."

Zach nodded. "Same as me. I was creeping up on one of them, and that Megan girl rolls off a rock and bang, I'm dead."

"Me too," Randy agreed. "I saw the tips of somebody's shoes poking out from under a tree. I sneak up to zap him, but it turns out no one's wearing them. She was just airing her smelly feet or something."

"Megan got you?" I asked, raising one eyebrow and giving Kurt a smirk.

"Yeah, total fluke."

"Ummm." I gave an exaggerated nod. "Sure sounds that way."

Kurt's eyes narrowed angrily. "Big deal if she knows how to handle a paint gun. Who wants to go out with a girl like that anyway? She'd probably want to arm wrestle you for the check."

Zach and Randy bobbed their heads.

"Talk about emasculating," Zach added. "*Yech!* I want a girl who knows how to be a girl."

"Same here," Randy agreed. "She's strictly not my type."

"You guys have got to be kidding," I said. "What if a girl isn't some kind of a priss?"

"Then she'd better go back to Feminine Training 101," Kurt barked. "Because nobody wants to hang with some Amazonian man hater."

I hooked my gun strap over my arm and scrambled over a large rock. "Just because a girl is good at sports and stuff doesn't make her a man hater."

"Oh yeah?" Kurt asked, climbing after me. "Why else do you think she'd do all that stuff? You didn't see any of the other girls squirming through the mud to make a shot."

I turned to stare at him. "So what?"

"So," Kurt hurled back. "It's obvious, isn't it? She knows she's hopeless. No guy in his right mind would ever want to run his hands through her ugly red hair or kiss her fat little cheek. She's got nothing to lose by trying to show guys up."

Not trusting my voice, I raised my hand to say *stop*. I slammed my gun into Kurt's arms and then quickly headed off down the path toward our cabin. He could return my stuff. And if he knew what was good for him, he'd stay out of my way for a while.

Part of me realized Kurt and the guys were only letting off steam because Megan had creamed us. But if I'd had to listen to another minute of them mocking her out, there was going to be another color on their black jumpsuits. Red. And it wasn't going to be paint!

Fifteen

Megan

"Well, that wasn't such a bad way to spend a Saturday night," I said, slightly sarcastically, as I hung up my paddle on the rec room's paneled wall. "Twenty-five games of Ping-Pong must be a world record. Maybe we should start a league."

"Was that what we were doing?" Serena laughed. "I thought we were practicing to become ball girls at the U.S. Open. All we did was chase down errant shots." She motioned at Laurie with her chin.

"Hey, I did my best," Laurie complained. "I never said I was a sports phenom like you two. I got the ball to land on the table a couple of times."

"Yeah," Serena joked. "Only on the wrong table!"

129

I scooped up the remaining balls and dropped them in the basket under the paddles.

We were the last three in the rec room—a small, boxy cabin with two Ping-Pong tables, three pinball machines, and not much else. Not exactly the hot spot to be, especially since—somewhere out there—the not-so-secret game of spin the bottle was going on at this very minute.

I was grateful to my girlfriends for skipping the game to keep me company. They didn't even have to ask me why. Serena and Laurie knew chapter and verse about my sixth-grade STB fiasco in Johnny Kerr's basement. And I'd made it perfectly clear that the spectacle of Ben and Alyssa in a lip lock was the last thing I wanted a front-row seat to.

"I'm not really that bad, am I?" Laurie asked, her glasses glinting in the fluorescent light.

I wrapped my arm around her shoulders and squeezed. "Don't worry. We'll make a jock out of you yet."

"Not likely." Serena snorted. She turned and snapped off the lights to the rec room, plunging us into darkness.

"Whoa!" I cried, feeling for the wooden banister that would let me safely navigate the stairs. It took a moment for my eyes to adjust to the darkness.

"Eerie," Laurie whispered, coming up behind me. "What's that noise?"

"Crickets?" I said, biting my lip.

"More like lions and tigers and bears!" Serena

joked, flipping on her flashlight. She scanned the area, catching the glittering eyes of a raccoon in the light. He seemed to be looking right at us for a second. Then he turned and disappeared into the woods.

"Yikes!" I gasped. "I bet there *are* bears out there."

Serena held the flashlight under her chin. "And ghosts."

"What's got her acting so brave?" Laurie asked, clutching my arm.

"Alex took her camping for two weeks last summer, remember?" I told Laurie. Serena's older brother, Alex, was a wilderness guide. "I think he scared all the fright out of her!"

Serena laughed. "Come on. We don't even need the flashlight. Look at the stars."

It was true. Once we were into the clearing, the night stars had the sky lit up like a neon sign. We could easily follow the path from the brightness of the moon. I took a deep breath. The air was crisp and cool with dew. "Beautiful," I whispered.

"This is where I leave you," Serena said, tapping her flashlight against the sign pointing to cabin B. "Are you guys going to be all right?"

We nodded, making brave sounds, but Laurie immediately began clutching my arm again.

Serena smirked. "Keep following the path through the clearing. A few yards later there's a fork. Take a left for cabin A, right for cabin C. You guys will be fine."

Gulp! That sounded good in theory. But one step out of the clearing and the overhanging tree-tops had us engulfed in darkness.

"It sure is quiet," Laurie whispered, sticking close to me as we walked. "Do you think anyone's around, you know, to rescue us?"

I gave a nervous laugh and checked the glowing dials on my watch. Ten-fifteen. "Probably. They can't all be in bed, right?"

Laurie nodded. "Unless the STB game broke up."

I swallowed as branches began to catch at my T-shirt and shorts and whip across my bare calves. "I really didn't want anything to do with that stupid game," I said, my voice wavering slightly, "but now I wouldn't mind if one of the players sort of wandered our way."

"You've got that right," Laurie seconded me. "Though what they'd be doing out here is anyone's guess."

I shuddered. We were way deep in the woods, without even a semblance of a path. If we were in the movies, this was when they would cut to the stalking psycho!

"Ow," Laurie whimpered. "That last branch smacked me right in the face. Maybe we should start screaming for help."

"Wait!" I cried. "What's that?"

"I don't know," Laurie gasped, "but I'm not going to wait around to find out." She crouched, ready to bolt.

"No, don't go." I grabbed her arm. "It's a build-ing. I think it's the canoe hut."

"Thank goodness!" she cried. "At least we'll be back on a trail."

We hurried around the side of the building, looking for the path. *Uh-oh!* Suddenly we were caught in the glow of a kerosene lantern.

"What the . . . ," I started to say.

"Looks like we found the game," Laurie whispered.

A group of about twelve people were sitting around in a circle. The participants would have headed the who's-who list at Hartley High. Which of course included Ben and Alyssa.

Please, God, I thought. *Put me back in the forest!* Lions and tigers and bears I could deal with. Seeing Alyssa sitting cross-legged next to Ben was another story.

Alyssa gave me a sickly sweet smile and waved us over. "Just in time! Come on, join the game."

Keep cool, I told myself, biting my lip. *We'll be out of this in a sec.* "Thanks, but we don't want to interrupt. Just taking a nighttime stroll. We'll be on our way."

Alyssa jumped to her feet. "Not so fast." There was a slight edge to her voice. "Surely you don't ex-pect us to believe you were just wandering around out here. Don't you like who you see?"

I started to protest, but Alyssa cut me off. "Or maybe you're just spying on us. What's the matter? Afraid of actually kissing someone?"

A few of the girls in the group giggled, and I could feel the skin on my face heating up.

"Maybe they don't feel like playing," Ben

growled. "Not everyone's into kids' games."

My eyes locked with Ben's, and I felt a shudder run down my spine, but what was he trying to say?

Alyssa turned and smiled at him. "Megan loves all the *other* games. If I'd never kissed a boy, I guess I'd be nervous too."

I could sense Laurie quaking by my side. I felt like that myself, but I wasn't going to let on to Alyssa. How dare she accuse me of never having been kissed—even if it was the truth.

I gave Laurie an I'm-sorry look and turned back to the group. "Then you're wrong," I said, willing my voice not to crack. "We'll stay for one spin. But after that we've got to go." *After all,* I tried to reassure myself, *what are the odds that the bottle will land on either of us with only one spin?*

"Great!" Alyssa clapped. "It was my turn, but since you're only staying for one spin . . ." She bent down and retrieved the bottle, holding it out toward me. "You can do the honors."

Oh no. What were those odds again? What have I gotten myself into?

"Come on, Megan." Alyssa twisted the bottle back and forth. "Don't chicken out now."

I took it reluctantly and joined the circle between Kurt and Jordan. *Please don't let this be a disaster,* I thought. *Please let me get out of this with a shred of dignity.*

I glanced at Laurie. She was sitting huddled between Jake Eisner and Paul Henley, looking almost as miserable as I felt.

I took a deep breath and gave the bottle a hard

spin. My palms were sweaty, and I clenched my teeth as the bottle circled the ground. *Not Kurt, please. Not Jordan. Not Jake. Not Paul. Not Kenny.* There wasn't one guy sitting there I wanted to kiss. Except Ben. But of all of the guys, he was the very last one I wanted the bottle to land on. Being rejected by or even having to experience the humiliation of a dry, grudging kiss from one of those guys would be nothing next to how I would feel if Ben rejected me.

I watched, my heart in my throat, as the bottle slowed down, bumping over the last stone until it finally rested at . . . *Ben!*

For a moment everyone sat in tense silence. I didn't dare to sit up on my knees. I didn't dare to lean closer. I couldn't bear to have Ben push me away. I closed my eyes, waiting for the mocking laughter to start—the cold, empty air teasing my frozen lips.

But suddenly I sensed the empty space around me filling up. Warm breath tickled my nose. Strong arms encircled my body. I blinked, looking up to see Ben's warm, hazel eyes smiling down at me. His handsome face coming closer until his soft, moist lips pressed longingly against mine.

Ben

Wow! I thought as my lips explored Megan's. *I've kissed a lot of girls in my time, but it's never felt like*

135

this before. I felt hot and dizzy, and there was a tingling running from the tips of my ears to my toes. I was dimly aware of the laughter and oohing from the other kids, but it was as if their sounds were coming from miles away. The whole world seemed to have shrunk to one tiny pinpoint, and that was Megan's full, soft mouth. With her nestled in my arms, our lips passionately locked together, there was nothing else that mattered.

"All right, people!" a loud voice boomed. "Everybody stays right where they are. I want names, and I want them now!"

Wha . . . ? My eyes snapped open, and Megan and I pulled apart. *We're busted!* Mr. Paisley, our hulking science teacher/camp chaperon, was hovering above us, his meaty fists on his hips, his dark, beetled brows turned down into two angry slashes.

Kurt doused the kerosene lantern, and the girls began to scream, with everyone scrambling to their feet and heading off into the woods.

I jumped up, and Alyssa grabbed my arm.

"Ben," she cried, tugging at me, "this way. Hurry!"

I shrugged her off and reached down to help Megan up. "C'mon," I said, "let's get out of here."

Megan smiled as I pulled her to her feet. We set off across the path, flying through the woods, laughing as we left Mr. Paisley's threatening shouts and everyone else far behind us. We didn't stop until we reached the clearing outside Megan's cabin, collapsing against a fallen tree to catch our breath.

"That was a close one," I panted, gulping for air. "Did you see the look on old man Paisley's face? I thought he was going to bust a gut."

Megan laughed, her eyes shining, her skin glistening in the moonlight. "Do you think we'll get in trouble?"

"I don't know." I stared at her dancing eyes and warm, rose pink lips and felt my heart swell in my chest. "But you know what—I don't care." I brushed a strand of silky red hair from her face. "Do you?"

She smiled and bit her lip. "No."

I felt this goofy grin stretch across my face. All I wanted to do was look at her. Be with her. I felt like a ten-year-old with my first crush. But tickling at the edges of my consciousness was this uneasy feeling. Already I could hear the other kids getting closer, the noise of their feet as they trampled through the underbrush, threatening to ruin this perfect moment.

I have to let her know how I feel, I thought. *And I have to do it now.* But there was so much I needed to explain. What happened at Jordan's party, for starters. How Kurt and my gang were pulling me one way but my heart was pulling me another. That Alyssa wasn't my girlfriend, even though my clique was acting like our coupledom was a done deal. *But where do I start?* My thoughts were like a jigsaw puzzle—too many pieces.

"Megan," I started to say. "I tried to call . . ." I stopped. They were out of the woods and on the path now. Only a few minutes left. I took a deep breath. "Alyssa and I . . ."

She stared back at me. I could feel her willing me to go on.

"Our friends think we should . . ."

Megan's eyes grew dark, and she looked down at her lap.

"They keep pushing us. But I don't . . ."

I could feel her turning away. I was making a total mess of this. And now I recognized the voices coming up the trail—Kurt, Tanya . . . Alyssa.

"Megan."

She turned her eyes back to mine—they were sad, and some of the light had gone out. There was only one way I could make her understand now. I pulled her close for another deep kiss—hoping my lips could convey even a fraction of what I was feeling.

"Ahem!" Kurt cleared his throat loudly.

I jumped, practically pushing off Megan to get to my feet. I hadn't realized they were *that* close. Kurt, Tanya, and Alyssa stood with crossed arms, staring at us. Megan gave a small yelp and flew into her cabin.

"I thought the game broke up fifteen minutes ago," Alyssa said in tight-lipped fury. Before I could respond, Kurt got me in a not-so-friendly headlock and began dragging me back to our cabin.

Sixteen

Megan

My lips were still tingling from Ben's kisses when I climbed into my bunk bed in the far corner of the cabin—but so were my arms from where he'd pushed me away. I dropped my head onto my pillow and closed my eyes against the dim cabin lights. My mind was a swirling mess. *What is he trying to say to me? What do his kisses mean?*

All around the cabin the other girls were whispering excitedly about the STB game being busted. And who had kissed who and when. Even girls who hadn't been there seemed to know every detail. I even heard Ben's name a couple of times attached to a lot of giggles.

I yanked my covers to my chin. It was almost as if Ben was two people. One way when his friends were around but someone else entirely when he was alone with me. *So who is the real Ben Donovan?*

"I heard Mr. Paisley's so mad, he's talking about a week's detention," Jennifer Park called out.

"Detention!" Gloria Coles countered. "Try suspension. As soon as he can figure out who was there."

"You should have seen the look on Tanya's face when Kurt's spin landed on that new cheerleader." Elizabeth Park, Jennifer's twin sister, giggled.

Gloria laughed. "I thought she was going to slap him for sure."

At that moment the door to our cabin swung open with a bang, and Alyssa stalked into the room. Her angry blue eyes lit on mine for a second before she focused on the rest of our cabin mates.

"Oh, please, you're not all yakking about that STB game, are you? That was child's play." She made a dismissive motion with her hand. "The real game started way before that." She paused dramatically. "A very select group of us played a private game of truth or dare right after dinner. Believe me, I could tell you all a thing or two that would knock your socks off."

Alyssa began to hum—dangerously close to my bunk—as she changed out of her tight tank top and hip-hugger shorts into a cotton nightie.

The rest of the room was completely silent now, each girl waiting for Alyssa to go on.

"Oh, all right." She sighed. Her eyes swept her captive audience, and her lips curled into a grin that would have made the Grinch proud. "We've all been sworn to secrecy, so I can't tell you the very best parts, but seeing that we're all roomies here, I'll let you in on one little tidbit." She began to giggle, and I could feel the shrillness of it running through me like nails on a blackboard.

"I dared a 'certain someone' to kiss the grossest girl on the trip. And," she added in a stage whisper, "he did it!"

I felt like the air had been sucked out of the room. I couldn't believe the other girls could be using their lungs for laughter. Begging Alyssa to tell them more when I could barely breathe. *Could she mean? Could he have actually . . .*

I turned over in my bunk, pressing my nose practically against the paneled wall, willing her to stop, willing them all to go to sleep, willing my tears not to fall. *Ben, did you really kiss me on a dare?*

Alyssa let loose another shrill laugh, and I pressed the pillow around my ears, trying desperately to drown out her words. *Not a chance.* It was impossible to miss the telltale creak of the top bunk right beside mine. We were now barely six feet apart.

"And how about those ridiculous games today?" Alyssa carried on. Her bunk had become her throne, with all her loyal subjects gathering around her. "Talk about a waste of time. I feel sorry for those pitiful tomboys who are *so* into it. It's pathetic that there are girls our age who actually think guys will be interested in them when they get all icky and sweaty. They're making total fools of themselves. Someone should say something, but they're probably too stupid to get it. Dumb and a jock. Forgivable in a guy—maybe even preferable in a guy." She tittered knowingly. "But in a girl you just have to laugh. They're such easy marks."

Alyssa made a kissing sound with her lips, and I felt like acid was flooding my veins, burning holes in my heart. *Ben, no . . .*

"I, for one, know that's not what it takes to get a guy," Alyssa continued. "I'm an ace swimmer, but I would never beat a man I was looking to snag at swimming. Only a major, clueless idiot would do something like that. But then, I guess that pretty much sums up jocky girls—clueless idiots. Do they actually think guys find that attractive?"

I was frozen on the outside but writhing in pure agony on the inside. Finally the lights went out, and the girls settled down. *Safe.* I could no longer hold back the tears. They flowed like hot lava from my eyes, seeping into my pillow as my shoulders shuddered under the blankets, my hand tight across my mouth to keep from sobbing out loud. *Ben's kisses felt so real.* Could I actually have been that naive and stupid?

Ben

"Jeez! Give it a rest," I hollered, stalking out of our cabin to give my ears a break. Ever since Kurt had come upon Megan and me, he'd been like a broken record. *Megan this. Alyssa that.* You would

142

think he was arguing about saving the planet or something.

Kurt was right on my heels, leaping down from the steps to confront me. "I would, Donovan, if I believed you were hearing one half of what I'm saying!"

"Me?" I looked at him incredulously. "I heard everything you said. You think I should date Alyssa because she's the in-crowd's darling and ignore Megan because she's a little overweight. Well, I like Megan, and I think Alyssa is a drag! End of story!"

Kurt threw up his hands. "Have you been taken over by aliens or what? Alyssa is the hottest babe at Hartley High. She's pure perfection. Megan isn't even from the same species as Alyssa. She's some fat girl who wriggled under your skin. Don't ask me how."

"Enough!" I spat, giving him a hard shove. "You're out of line here. Not another word about Megan!"

Kurt stumbled backward into a pine tree, catching himself on a branch seconds before he tumbled over. My fists were up, ready for a fight.

But instead of coming at me, he took a deep breath. He seemed to be considering his words carefully for a moment. His brow was furrowed in concentration. Finally he looked over at me and smiled. "You know, you're right." He shook his head. "That wasn't fair." Kurt walked back to the cabin steps and took a seat. "Megan's probably a great kid. And I shouldn't slam your friends."

"Good," I said, "that's resolved. Now I'm going to bed." I started to step over him to reach the cabin door, but he caught my pant leg.

"Just one thing."

I gritted my teeth. I knew it was too much to hope that he would give up so easily. But he was wasting his breath. Nothing he could say against Megan would make me change my mind. I stepped back onto the dirt path, glaring at him. "Shoot, but make it quick. This subject is dead as a dodo bird as far as I'm concerned."

Kurt ran a hand through his dark brown hair. "When do you plan to take her home for dinner?"

Kurt couldn't have done a better job of knocking the air out of my lungs if he had used his fists. I immediately began to imagine Megan meeting my father and stepmother. It wasn't pretty. In my mind's eye I saw Megan walking into the living room. A quick cut to my father's disapproving sniff, the patronizing smile that didn't quite reach his eyes, and then my stepmother's raised eyebrow and decided silence as they gave her the once-over.

Nothing would be said at the time; they would be perfectly charming. Megan would even think she was making a good impression, but it would be anything but. The dissection would start as soon as she left the house—bit chunky, not a member of the country club, no social connections. *Three strikes, she's out.* The conclusion: NOKD. *Not our kind, dear.*

"I'm only trying to do you both a favor," Kurt added quietly, studying his fingernails. "Seems to me you're being pretty selfish and setting her up for a big-time hurt in the process."

I stared down at the dirt path, rolling a rock back and forth with the toe of my hiking boot. "What do you mean by that?"

"She'll fall in love with you, but you won't be able to properly date her. She'll never be accepted by your family or your friends. She'll be a pariah. I know you, Ben. You're a social being. After a while you'll have to make a choice—her or everyone else that ever mattered to you."

I flinched. I really liked Megan, but who knew if she was the love of my life? Did I care about her enough to risk losing all my friends, and piss off my father and Eve, to find out?

Kurt started a little tooth-assisted surgery on his cuticle. "I'm afraid to say it, but you're not doing Megan any favors either. Alyssa was pretty ballistic. She doesn't like being crossed. I think I was able to get you off the hook by telling her it was just a mercy kiss. But I'll warn you now—if you don't quit hanging out with Megan, Alyssa and Tanya and the other girls are going to make her life miserable."

I sank down on the stairs next to Kurt and closed my eyes. *Why is this so hard?* I wondered. *Why is everything and everyone against us?* All I'd wanted to do was spend some time with Megan and get to know her. I liked her—a lot. But if everyone was intent on attacking our budding relationship, how could it survive? I felt my shoulders sag. With so much going against us, maybe for Megan's sake—and my own—I should forget all about her.

Seventeen

Megan

Oh *no!* I thought. *This can't be happening.* But sure enough, the camp's head rafting guide was pointing right at me. I was safely squeezed in next to Serena in the big blue rubber raft.

"Megan," he said, from his position on the muddy bank of the river. "There are too many campers in that boat. You've got to go back to the raft you were assigned to. That's the red one at the front of the line."

I winced, clutching at the handles on the side of the boat. There was no way in this lifetime I was going to set foot in the red boat. Only the most demonic twist of fate could have resulted in my having to share a raft with Tanya and Kurt, Alyssa and . . . Ben.

Until I'd come down to the riverbank this morning, I'd still been holding on to the slim hope that Alyssa's words last night had been a lie. But by the way Ben acted when I arrived, the cool way he ignored me, I knew the only liar was my heart—saying he still cared.

"There's got to be some kind of mistake," I whispered. "Can't I just stay here?"

"There's no mistake," the guide bellowed. "Says right here"—he tapped at the list of names on his clipboard—"Megan Kennedy, raft one. That's that one." He stabbed his pencil in the direction of the red raft from hell. "*My* boat."

"I'll go," Serena said. "I'll switch places with her."

The guide shook his head. "Against policy. The rafts are assigned. Each person wears a color-coded bracelet in case of accidents. If you two switch, everyone else is going to want to switch also. We'd have mayhem. A total breakdown in safety standards. I'm not taking any chances."

Serena gave me a piteous look. "I'm sorry, Megs," she whispered.

I stepped onto the shore like a condemned man. But I had one more trick up my sleeve. "I'm going to give this a skip," I said in a faltering voice. "I'm feeling a little queasy."

The guide fixed me with his piercing blue eyes. "No can do. Nobody gets left behind on my watch. Once we're on the water, you'll forget all about not being with your friends."

"Megan, take your place," Mr. Paisley hollered. "We haven't got all day."

"C'mon, Megan," my classmates called out. "Stop trying to ruin our fun. Let's go!"

I looked at my antsy classmates and out at the silvery blue water. Unless I planned to drown myself, I didn't have much choice. I reluctantly walked down the muddy bank and climbed into the torture vessel—banished to the back, where I would sit shotgun opposite the guide's position.

Kurt, Tanya, Alyssa . . . and Ben. None of them paid me any mind. I was like the invisible woman—the foursome stared straight through me.

The steely-eyed guide leaned over our raft and began handing out paddles and life preservers.

"Ugh," Alyssa said, holding the orange flotation device disdainfully between two fingers. "What am I supposed to do with this?"

"Wear it," the guide barked. "These waters can be extremely dangerous. Especially in the late spring. We had a lot of snow this winter and a lot of rain last week."

Alyssa snickered as she pointed to the perfectly still river. "I don't think so. And I didn't wear this itsy-bitsy bikini to cover it up with a gross, smelly life preserver. I want a nice, even tan."

"We're not going anywhere until you put it on," the man shot back before turning to confer with two of the other guides standing by the side of the river.

That was my cue to get out of the boat. I pretended

to be stretching my legs. But the truth was, sitting in that raft, getting the ice-out treatment from Ben and his friends, was way too painful. After all the tears I'd cried last night, I didn't think there could be any left. *Wishful thinking!* I could feel them churning right at the surface of my lids.

I took a deep breath and concentrated on the guides. I didn't like the uneasy looks that were passing between them. *Something's not right,* I thought.

The guides were huddled close to each other and whispering in low voices. I only caught a little of what they said, but I knew that *cfs* was rafters' lingo for cubic feet per second. In other words, a way to measure the intensity of the river. And from the numbers they were throwing around, it sounded like this class-I beginner's trip was morphing into a class-V expert one! I inched closer.

"Don't worry," I heard the head guide whisper. "As long as you get them to pull very hard for river left and run the chute between Demon's Boulder and Hammerhead Hole, you'll stick to Lady's Slipper. They'll never even know Devil's Gulch exists."

Devil's Gulch! I gulped. My dad had told me stories about Devil's Gulch—with its nosedive down a mind-boggling gradient to galloping rapids of ever-escalating intensity. Not a place I would like to face in a boat full of amateurs. *This guide better know what he's doing!*

Our leader returned to the raft, and I quickly scrambled on board. He frowned at Alyssa with gritted teeth. "Put that life jacket on at once!"

"C'mon, Alyssa," Kurt said. "Now *you're* holding up the works."

"Fine!" She shrugged into it, but that was as far as she would go. Alyssa categorically refused to link the thick black straps across her chest.

As we pushed off from the bank, I tried to train my eyes on the gorgeous scenery around us—the wildflowers blanketing the shore, giving way to steep, granite cliffs that towered majestically above us. Anything to avoid the sight of Kurt and Tanya cuddling on the left side of the raft and Ben and Alyssa sitting side by side on the right.

As we drifted lazily along, our guide began to run down the rules for the trip. "We do this as a team," he said. "Everyone paddles at the same time. If we pull to the right, I'll tell the right side to ease up and the left side will paddle alone. If we pull to the left, same thing until we straighten out. I'll be navigating from the back. We'll start on the count of two. One, two."

The raft veered to the right as everyone started to paddle except Alyssa. She turned to the guide, flashing a bright smile. "Sorry, but I can't paddle. I have an audition for a hand-modeling assignment next week. My agent says no calluses. Ben will have to do the work for both of us." She snuggled up alongside him.

I felt my heartache giving way to anger. *Make me gag!* How could he stand a girl like that? How could he have kissed me the way he did last night—on a dare or not—and then let Alyssa crawl all over him today?

I started to turn my eyes away in disgust as Ben shifted in his seat. *Wait a sec.* Was he shifting toward her or away from her? I couldn't help thinking that Ben wasn't looking altogether comfortable with Alyssa hanging on him. *Is it my imagination, or does he look . . . trapped?*

Before I could make sense of what I was feeling, I heard Tanya give a terrified gasp. I looked at the water before us. The calm, rippling river was quickly turning into a turbulent, surging swirl.

"Keep paddling! To the left! To the left!" the guide hollered over the crashing sound of white water.

But I could see he'd miscalculated. We were cutting the raft too late and too tight. Instead of heading down the leisurely scenic line of Lady's Slipper we were plunging right into Devil's Gulch!

I hunkered down, but what help would that be—I was staring up at a massive wall of water about to crash over us! I held my breath, bracing my legs and clinging to the side of the boat, hoping I wouldn't be thrown into the churning current as the swell washed over us.

Ker-crash! I opened my eyes, spitting out water. I

was safe—still on the raft. But where was our guide? I turned to see him pulling himself out of the water onto the riverbank from ten feet behind us! He shouted for us to turn around, but at that moment we were hit by two more massive waves, sending us into a spiral that left our bow pointing upstream. We were shooting down Devil's Gulch backward!

Alyssa and Tanya started screaming their heads off. Kurt turned a sickly green. Ben was keeping his cool, but I could see the fear in his eyes. This was life or death, and I knew what I had to do. I threw off my feelings of self-consciousness and inferiority and leaped to the guide's post.

"Paddle right! Right!" I screamed. "Kurt! Tanya! Wake up! Paddle right!"

No response. Tanya and Alyssa, their voices hoarse, were cowering in the bottom of the raft, and Kurt was retching over the side.

Ben leaped to the left, shoving Kurt out of the way. "Tell me what to do, Megan!"

"Up!" I barked. "Ride the high side right! Paddle toward the eddy, by the boulder!" I pointed straight ahead to where a large boulder was jutting out into the water.

Ben paddled furiously, synchronizing his motion with mine. Our only chance was to get the raft around the downriver side of that boulder— out of the grinding, crashing current. A barrier, like a boulder, would often form a relatively quiet pool on one side. The problem was we had to avoid being pasted to the rock like a postage stamp. If we got stuck on the wrong side of the boulder, the savage current could flip the raft and flush us all into the water.

Almost there! Inches from the safety of the big rock we bumped against a smaller boulder, and Kurt was pitched over the side. He screamed and flailed as he was sucked down by the foam-filled rapids. He came up about six feet from the raft, floating on his back and spitting out water. "Help!" he sobbed. "Help me!"

Think fast, Kennedy, I told myself. *Do you want to save Kurt or keep the rest of the crew safe?* The eddying current had pushed us safely to the other side of the big rock. We could have waited there until help came. But without Kurt. He would be heading downriver, on the ride of his soon-to-be short life. But if I pushed off the boulder to go after him, the rest of us would be thrown back into the most violent rapids on Redwing River, with somersaulting waves and enormous sucking holes. I couldn't navigate it all by myself.

I locked eyes with Ben. The electricity crackled between us. In that split second—without a word spoken—I knew Ben understood. We *would* get down this river—together. I gripped my paddle and pushed off the big rock with all my might. We shot out of the boulder's protective zone and into the soup. Ben's arm snaked out and grabbed the collar of Kurt's life jacket, hauling him into the raft.

Our eyes met once more, and we both smiled. Then Ben took his place by my side. United, we were ready to tackle the stampeding, savage white water that was looming before us.

Ben

"Not again!" I gasped, my heart in my throat. Right up ahead was another series of gnashing, foam-filled eruptions of white water. I was exhausted. *Megan must be nearly dead,* I thought.

Megan's eyes were the size of two round globes. "Looks like a bad one," she muttered. "Hold on to your oar."

Tanya and Alyssa whimpered from the floor of the raft. Kurt was on the side, his hands clenched around his oar in a death grip.

"Hey!" Alyssa shrieked. She pointed to a spot right past the churning water. "People!"

I squinted through the spray and could make out a group of picnickers waving their arms by the side of the river.

"It's the take-out spot!" Megan cried. "All we have to do is make it past these next rapids, and we're home free!"

"Hallelujah!" I pumped my fist in the air, grinning wildly at Megan. Every cell in my body wanted to take her in my arms, spin her around, and kiss her with all the passion in my being.

I am madly in love with her! I realized. Maybe it

had taken the most intense experience of my life to get that through my thick skull, but I wouldn't waste any more time about it now. In a hundred feet, when we were safely onshore, I was going to tell her just that!

Megan laughed, her eyes bright with excitement, looking radiant with her wild red hair and wind-whipped pink cheeks. She leaned her head close to mine. Right then I would have kissed her, but her eyes turned grave.

"We're not there yet," she whispered, keeping her voice low so as not to alarm the others. "But we'll get through this. Follow my lead."

No problem, I thought. *The sooner we get to shore, the sooner my lips will be locked with yours.*

Megan started with shallow paddles toward the right, motioning for me and Kurt to do the same. We skirted a large boulder and immediately the river began to look like it was boiling.

"Hang on!" she warned.

Instantly we were sucked into the rapids' frothy, bubbling cauldron.

"Left!" she screamed. "High side the left!"

I leaped to the right side of the raft, paddling frantically to keep us on course.

"Whoa!" I howled as the boat plunged down a steep drop.

Tanya, Alyssa, and Kurt opened their mouths, their hoarse screams lost in the water's rumble.

Megan leaned over so far on the side, I had to clutch her life jacket to keep her from tumbling over. She straightened and dug in her oar. "We've got to pivot," she shouted. "But I don't have the strength."

I grabbed her oar, and she caught mine. I leaned down with all my weight, and she furiously paddled us around my pole.

"We did it!" she cried as the boat shot toward shore and safely out of the rapids. The people on the riverbank erupted into whoops and hollers.

Alyssa and Tanya began waving from the raft. Kurt wore a sheepish grin.

We were gliding into shore, my eyes locked with Megan's, my words of love on the tip of my tongue, when suddenly we hit a bump.

"Help!" Alyssa cried, flipping out of the raft— the life jacket she'd refused to strap on slipping off. "I can't swim!"

For a split second we all stared at her flailing arms, too shocked to do anything. But then like a heavy rock, she disappeared under the surface of the water.

No time to think, Ben! I dove over the side and pulled her up from the bottom of the river. It wasn't very deep, but for a nonswimmer even a puddle could be fatal. Who knew how much water she'd taken into her lungs? She needed CPR, pronto! I hooked Alyssa around her arms and dragged her out of the water onto the riverbed.

Her eyes were closed, and she didn't seem to be breathing. Tanya, Kurt, Megan, and the picnickers crowded around us. I pinched Alyssa's nose and put my lips against hers, ready to push in the air that would bring her back to life.

What? Suddenly Alyssa's arms snaked around my neck. Her lips went from limp to hungry. She was kissing me!

I heard Megan's gasp like a gunshot going off inside my brain. I turned, struggling to get out of Alyssa's grasp. But not quick enough. I only caught sight of the back of Megan's sodden T-shirt as she raced up the steep path away from the river.

Eighteen

Megan

"Tell us about your wild rafting trip, Megs!" Linda Beller gushed as she set up the volleyball for Danny Lui.

"I'm all talked out," I growled, crouching down to return Danny's spike. I expertly knocked the ball back onto their side. I'd been pestered with questions about the white-water ride for the past hour, and I was sick of it. I was concentrating on sports now—a pickup game of volleyball—while we waited for the dinner bell. The trip had turned into a total disaster, and I didn't want to be reminded of it.

"C'mon, Megs," Lisa Craft urged. She missed an easy shot, and I ran to retrieve the ball. "I heard that except for Ben, everyone else was useless," she called after me. "I heard you single-handedly got the raft down the rapids."

"And then Alyssa almost drowned!" Sandi Clifford chimed in.

"Yeah," I uttered gruffly, trotting back to the net, "funny how she forgot she was an ace swimmer."

"Lucky Ben knew CPR," Sandi mused. "That must have been some kiss."

Slam! I smashed the volleyball as hard as I could. Of all the underhanded, devious, low-life girlie tricks I'd ever seen . . .

"Whoa! Megs," Sandi called out from across the volleyball net. "Easy. We're trying to play a friendly game here, not kill each other."

"Sorry," I snarled. But could I help it if I kept seeing Alyssa's smug face superimposed on the volleyball? I took a deep breath and dropped down to my knee for Danny's next spike. I got my hands under the ball and set up Lisa, who faked a spike and pushed it back to me. *Wham!* I rocketed the ball over the net, sending the other side scattering.

"Megs!"

"Sorry. My hand slipped," I shouted back. *I wish my hands could slip around something else,* I thought darkly. *Like Alyssa's scrawny neck.* I wiped the beads of sweat from my brow. That was our moment! I'd seen the love in Ben's eyes as we rode down those rapids. And then Miss Runner-up went and stole him away from me—again—with her fake drowning act.

"Yours!" Lisa called as Danny served. I threw myself to the side, getting under a ball that easily could have been called out. *Why not?* This was what I was good at. Playing sports was the only thing I could lose myself in. It was the best thing in the world.

"Can I play?"

I pivoted on my feet. Ben was standing by the side of the net, a hopeful look on his face.

"Yes, please," Sandi gasped. "I can't take any more of this. But watch out for Megan 'the Pulverizer' Kennedy. She's in rare form today."

Ben took his place across the net from me. He smiled sheepishly. I could practically see the apology forming on his lips. But how long would that last? Until the next damsel in distress cried "help"? Or until the next time Alyssa dropped her hankie?

The volleyball came his way, and he hit it back low and to the right in my direction. A soft shot— one that I could easily return for a score.

Wait a sec! Hadn't I learned anything from Alyssa's little trick . . . ?

Ben

Am I seeing right? I thought. *Megan must be really tired.* She was missing the easiest points.

I whacked the ball gently straight toward her, and it landed with a thud at her feet.

"Whoops!" She giggled, wriggling her fingers in the air. "You're too good for me!"

I narrowed my eyes. *I smell a rat,* I thought. My

161

little sister could have made that shot. Megan should have been all over it.

Megan picked up the ball and threw it weakly into the air. Her effort was so feeble that all she could do was tap it over the net.

Sandi, our weakest player, lobbed the ball back toward her in a gentle, slow-motion arc. But instead of knocking it back, Megan jumped out of the way with a squeal.

I wouldn't have believed it if I hadn't seen it with my own eyes. The heroine who had gotten us down the churning rapids was acting like she was afraid of a volleyball. *Acting.* Bingo! *But why?*

At that moment the dinner bell rang, and our game broke up. Megan picked up the volleyball and started toward the rec room to return it.

"Megan," I called, jogging after her. Maybe I would get an answer to that question now. But at the very least I wanted to ask her to be my date at tonight's fireworks.

She turned, and her eyelashes fluttered rapidly.

"Do you have something in your eye?" I asked.

"No." She giggled, cocking her head at a coy angle.

What in the world? I thought. This was even worse than her acting lame at sports. She was being totally un-Megan-like. Had she been hit on the head by the volleyball when my back was turned? "Um . . . Megan . . . ," I started.

"Yes, Ben?" she asked, her eyes doing that weird flutter thing again.

"Would you go to the fireworks with me tonight?"

"Of course!" she gushed, hugging the ball to her chest. "I'd love that more than anything."

"Pick you up at eight," I said, and sped out of there. Hopefully by tonight she would have snapped back to her senses. Otherwise I might be tempted to dribble that volleyball off her head a few times.

Megan

I can't believe playing girlie-girl actually worked! I thought as Ben and I walked toward the lake where the Redwing Mountain camp counselors were going to set off the Sunday-night fireworks. *But here I am, on a date—a real date—with Ben!*

"Hi, Megan. Hi, Ben." Voices greeted us as we walked along the path, looking for a spot with a good view. Since today's rafting incident Ben's friends, especially Kurt and Tanya, had been acting pretty nice to me. Well, at least acknowledging my existence. All except Alyssa, who was still throwing daggers at me with every look. *Though who can blame her?* I smiled to myself. *I'm beating her at her own game.*

Laurie and Serena were hanging out with a group of girls from the lacrosse team. They waved, and Serena gave me the thumbs-up sign as we passed. Ben hesitated, thinking I would want to stop.

163

"Oh, let's keep going," I whispered. "I bet we'll find a better place up ahead." I waved to the girls and kept moving. The truth was I didn't want my friends to see the way I was acting with Ben. Serena assumed we'd hooked up because of the wild rafting ride. I felt way too embarrassed to tell her the truth. *I got this date after I started using Alyssa tricks.*

The very thought of how I'd had to act to get the date sat like a sour cherry in my stomach. I couldn't help feeling I was walking by Ben's side under false pretenses. This Megan wasn't the real me. But as I glanced over at Ben, taking in his strong, clean profile and his broad, muscular shoulders, my cares fell away. Acting like a coy, girlish giggler was what had put me at his side, and as long as it kept me there, I wasn't about to change my approach.

"So, Megan," Ben started. "Which team do you think'll win the all-weekend trophy?"

"With just the water-volleyball contest left to-morrow"—I grinned—"is there any question? Team . . . I mean . . ." *What am I doing? First rule of being a girlie-girl—don't give your own opinions!* "I don't know." I smiled, discreetly batting my eyelashes. "What do you think?"

Ben gave me a sidelong glance. "I'd say team B."

"Team B?" I asked, staring at him incredu-lously. "Have you seen their starting lineup? This is water volleyball we're talking about." *Whoops!* "I mean, I . . . um . . . see what you mean. Good choice. Team B . . . sure . . . I can see that." I suppressed a shudder. I didn't like this at all. It felt like I was constantly stuffing a sock in my mouth or, worse, saying things that I didn't believe.

We reached the far edge of the lake, which unfortunately was also packed with people. Ben pulled me in the direction of the woods. "I know a great place. We need to cross a log over the creek, but then we've got a perfect view of the fireworks."

I stumbled after him until we reached the fallen tree, which was covered with moss. In my usual mountain attire—sneakers and shorts—scrambling across the log wouldn't have been any problem. But tonight I'd borrowed an adjustable silk wraparound skirt and a pair of platform sandals from one of the girls in my cabin. No way could I bushwhack in that kind of outfit.

"Ben," I said tentatively, in my most helpless voice. "Could we go back to the path? I'm afraid I'll get dirty." I crinkled my nose the way I'd seen Alyssa do.

Ben turned and squinted. I almost felt like he was studying me. I giggled nervously, hoping I wasn't failing the femininity test. He dropped his eyes. "Sure, Megan." He smiled. "Whatever you want." He held out his arm to guide me out of the woods.

I released a few more relieved giggles. *This is working like a charm,* I thought. *Sure, I can't exactly say*

I'm having any fun, but Ben's smiling. Isn't that what's most important?

Ben

I can't believe Megan's still acting like this, I thought. I glanced over—checking her out in the light of a Roman candle that glittered over the lake. The people around us *oohed* and *aahed.* She looked the same—long red hair, light brown eyes, and glowing skin. But she obviously hadn't snapped out of the weird head she'd been in since this afternoon's volleyball game. If I believed in alien abductions, I would have said she'd been subjected to some kind of brain experiment!

"Isn't this wonderful, Ben!" she enthused, doing a little hop in her high-heeled sandals. "I love fireworks! Everyone's having such a great time. But they're *so* scary."

She leaned toward me, and my arm automatically slipped around her shoulders as my mouth worked itself into yet another fake smile. "Yeah, sure," I said from between rigor-mortis lips. I'd been grinning like Politeness Man for so long, my jaw was sore.

"Scary stuff," I muttered. *Gimme a break!* First of all, these were camp fireworks—basically a bunch of bottle rockets that wouldn't have rated so much as a sigh at Hartley's annual Fourth of July celebration. On top of that, this was Megan.

A girl who could take you out with a volley of paint pellets at thirty yards. She would sooner be frightened of her own shadow than a couple of cheesy firecrackers.

Another round exploded in the air, and I hid a yawn with my hand before checking my watch. Nine-twenty. Ten more minutes before I could politely end this date.

I sighed. To be fair, this evening wasn't the worst I'd ever spent. In fact, it was pretty much like all the other dates I'd been on. *Which I guess is what's making this so hard to take,* I realized. Girls who gushed and giggled and acted like all they wanted to hear about was what *I* thought—I was used to that and way tired of it. Megan had seemed like something different, and that was the main reason I'd fallen for her. She was her own person—spunky, smart, and capable.

Hey, I know! A lightbulb went off in my head. *The rafting trip.* Maybe that would remind her of who she really was. I took a deep breath. "Megan, you were totally amazing today out on the river. I . . ."

Megan grabbed my arm, her eyes bright with excitement. "We couldn't have gotten down the rapids without you."

What? Was she patronizing me? "Without m-me?" I stammered. "You were the one . . ."

"You were so brave," she practically simpered, squeezing my biceps.

Oh, brother, I thought. If I closed my eyes, I could have been with Alyssa.

167

"Ooh, look, it's the finale!" she cried. "My father told me that's the time to make a wish."

"Ahhh!" the crowd murmured.

I tilted back my head to see an explosion of gold, blue, and red colored lights. I'd never heard about the wish business before. "But if it's true," I whispered to myself, "please, bring the real Megan back to me by morning."

Nineteen

Megan

"*Augh*," I groaned, smacking my fist against the palm of my hand. My teammate Diana Riis had just botched another easy assist, giving team D a nearly impossible to beat eight-point lead in the water-volleyball game. We'd sneaked past team C in the first round, but this game was for all the marbles. "Keep your eye on the ball," I called from the side of the pool.

"I can't, Megan," Diana shot back, practically in tears. "I'm lousy at this stupid game. You should be playing." She stamped her bare foot in the swimming pool, causing a small wave to splash the top of her blue, paisley bikini.

"C'mon, Megan," my other teammates called out. "Diana's right. We need you." Ryan,

Julia, and Chiara made frantic motions with their arms, waving me into the pool.

Even Ben was waving me in from our opponents' side of the net. *But what does he really mean?* I wondered.

I lowered my eyes and backed innocuously into the group of spectators. *Impossible.* If I played, I would blow my whole girlie-girl act.

Serena came up to me and gripped my arm. "Megs," she whispered, "get in there, girl. What's the matter with you? This is the last game before we get back on the bus to Hartley. If your team loses this, there's no way you're going to win the all-weekend trophy."

I bit my lip. "I don't feel well, remember?" I murmured. And it was true. I was seriously beginning to feel sick to my stomach. *Ugh!* I turned my eyes as Zach spiked another kill for team D. *12–2.* We were going down big time. Our team's only hope was . . . *me.*

Serena shook her head. "Pitiful. This game's wholesale slaughter." She glanced back at me and narrowed her dark eyes. "What's with the getup and the platform sandals? For someone who's not feeling well, you're looking pretty good."

I tugged on the hem of my yellow sundress. How could I tell my best friend that I'd chosen a fake me over the real one so I could have Ben? "Um . . . I've got my bathing suit on under this. I was going to play. It's just . . ."

Serena raised an eyebrow. "You're still hung up about everyone seeing you, right?"

I stared back at her, not saying a word.

Serena crossed her arms. "You think it's better to let your team down than let them see you with a little roll of fat."

"So what?" I shot back. "You know that about me. That's nothing new."

"But now people are depending on you, Megs. This isn't a beauty contest. Your teammates aren't going to see some fat girl wading out into the pool. They're going to see their heroine who's going to save the game for them. Same with the other side," she added. "They're going to be trembling in their swim trunks. Seeing the figure of their doom."

Not all of them, I thought. *Ben will be looking too.* But I couldn't tell Serena that. He would see a girl who was too strong for her own good. Who was nothing like the girls he went out with. He would realize I wasn't the docile, giggly type he'd asked out on last night's date. And then he'd never ask me out again.

"Suit yourself, Megs," Serena said, turning away. "I'll catch you back on the bus. I can't stand here and watch this massacre."

I looked hopelessly back at the pool. Team D was whooping it up on the far side of the net—splashing each other and kidding around. The score was so lopsided in their favor, they didn't even have to pretend to be serious. That got me mad. But what was I going to do? Protest? Hardly. I'd stay as meek as I'd been since Ben and I hooked up last night.

Yuck! I shuddered as my cutesy behavior at last night's fireworks came back to me. *But,* I quickly reminded myself, *it was worth the sacrifice.* Ben had been smiling. He'd had a good time. But then a stronger, louder voice shouted back in my brain, *I didn't! I had a lousy time!*

What am I doing? I thought. Suddenly I felt like a bolt of lightning had struck me. *Since when did I aspire to be a sniveling, self-denying wimp? Since never! That's not what I want to be!*

Okay, I'd wanted Ben for like a million years. But if the price of going out with him was not being me, then I couldn't afford it. I would rather be *me* without Ben than somebody else with him!

I charged to the edge of the pool, startling several bystanders. A space cleared out around me as my teammates—and everybody else, it seemed—looked at me expectantly. *It's now or never,* I thought.

I reached down and yanked my sundress over my head, revealing my new purple suit—and my new, take-no-prisoners attitude. "Team A rules!" I shouted, tossing the dress to one side and kicking off the platforms I'd been wearing. "Here comes the Annihilator!" And with that, I dove smoothly into the pool, ready to recapture the game for my team.

Ben

"All right!" I shouted as Megan spiked the ball hard over the net for her eighth kill of the game. "Awesome!"

"Hey, Donovan," my teammate Joe Dansker complained, "whose side are you on?"

I sheepishly looked around at my teammates. "Sorry." I blushed before treading into the deep end of the pool to retrieve the volleyball. *Rooting for the other team is not cool, Donovan,* I reminded myself. *But how can I help it?* It looked like Megan's bizarre amnesia attack was finally over. I was totally psyched that she was being herself again. *And* she looked unbelievably beautiful—curvaceous and totally confident—in her sizzling purple one-piece.

I tossed the ball to Zach, who executed a competent serve. But it seemed like Megan was everywhere at once. No sooner had the ball crossed the net than she exploded out of the water with a perfect block—setting up one of her teammates for a buzz-bomb spike. Having been up ten points, we were now tied at twelve in the decisive game. Things were looking grim.

Team A served, and Kurt got under it. His pass came my way, and I shot out of the water, pounding the ball for what looked like a surefire kill.

Surefire? Not with Megan there. *Slam! Wham! Shhh-bang!* It was all over in a matter of seconds.

Megan pulverized us for the last three points, leading team A to victory.

I could feel a mile-long grin stretching across my face as Megan pulled herself out of the pool. Her cheering teammates instantly surrounded her. I hopped out of the water next to her, big congratulations and an even bigger kiss for her on my lips. But as hard as I tried, I couldn't catch her eye. Every time I made a move to get closer to her, Megan would pull back into the throng of supporters. *It's as if she's trying to avoid me. But why?*

Serena raced up from the dirt path. "What's going on? What happened?" she cried, jumping up to try to look over the shoulders of the group.

I tapped Serena on the arm and grinned as she turned to face me. "Megan decided to play."

Serena laughed and clapped. She knew what that meant. "All right, Megs! But why are you standing back here? Can't congratulate the opposition?"

I shook my head. "Hey, I'm one of Megan's biggest fans. But . . ."

"What?" Serena asked me, her large, dark eyes probing mine.

I shrugged. "She won't even acknowledge me."

"Huh?" Serena said. "I don't get it. Did you two have words?"

I frowned, stepping back to avoid being run over by two more members of Megan's excited fan club.

"No, at least, I don't think so. A half hour ago she was waving to me from the sidelines, but since she dove into the pool to join the game, she won't even look at me."

Serena wrinkled her brow as if trying to make sense of what I'd said. "Oh!" She snapped her fingers. "I get it! And I thought she was hung up about the bathing suit."

"Bathing suit?" I asked. "Why? It's perfect. She looks like a total goddess."

Serena smiled, waving her hand in a dismissive motion. "Long story. But the dress, the platform sandals . . . Megs wasn't playing because she was trying to be like the girls you usually go out with. She doesn't think you like her anymore."

"What?" I blurted out. "I've been trying to tell her since yesterday that I'm crazy about her. But every time I open my mouth, she starts to giggle. Now she's back to normal, and she thinks *that's* what I don't like?"

Serena laughed, shaking her head. "Man! It's going to take weeks for you two to sort this thing out."

Weeks? Now that I'd finally found real love, I couldn't live without Megan for weeks. *Wait a minute!* I thought, scratching my chin. *I think I'll take a page out of another girl's playbook.*

"Serena, I've got an idea," I said, a smile sneaking across my face. "But I'm going to need your help." I leaned close and whispered my plan in her ear. "Okay?"

Serena winked. "You've got it!"

Splash! I threw myself backward into the deep end of the pool—kicking my feet to make sure I would sink to the bottom. I could hear Serena's muted cry from my watery position. "Omigod! Ben's fallen into the pool. He's hit his head!"

I had to suppress my laughter so I wouldn't take in a snootful of water. I opened my eyes to take a peek at the commotion at poolside. Serena did a body block to prevent Kurt from coming to my rescue. I couldn't help laughing at the sight, and a few bubbles escaped to the surface.

"Megan, quick," Serena cried as one of the camp's lifeguards blew his whistle and dove in. "Save him!"

I clamped my eyes shut when I heard the splash, knowing Megan had dived in too. I prayed she would reach me before the lifeguard did. Getting CPR from anybody but Megan would be gruesome.

When Megan's warm arms encircled my bare skin, I shivered slightly at her touch. I let her guide me to the surface. "I'm here, Ben," Megan whispered. "Please, hold on."

I played unconscious and allowed Megan, with Kurt and Jordan's help, to carry me to the grassy slope next to the cement patio surrounding the pool.

"You're going to be okay," Megan murmured, gently cradling my head in her hands. I could feel her breath warming my face as she lowered her

mouth toward mine to start mouth-to-mouth re-
suscitation. As soon as her lips touched mine, I
wrapped my arms around her. Her eyes widened in
shock, and she began to pull back. But I held on
tight.

"Don't be mad," I pleaded. "I'm too crazy about
you to play fair."

She blinked once. "You are?" I could hear the
trembling in her voice. "Me? Or . . . ?"

"You," I said hoarsely, my voice full of longing.
"The *real* you."

Megan's face turned from shocked white to
glowing pink. I pulled her tight against my chest,
and our lips met—gently at first and then more ur-
gently—until it felt like our bodies had melted together and the rest of the world had ceased to exist.

Do you ever wonder about falling in love? About members of the opposite sex? Do you need a little friendly advice but have no one to turn to? Well, that's where we come in . . . Jenny and Jake. Send us those questions you're dying to ask, and we'll give you the straight scoop on life and love.

DEAR JAKE

Q: *Dan's one of my closest friends, but he recently confessed to one of my girlfriends that he has a huge crush on me! I'm afraid that if we keep hanging out, I'll give him mixed signals about us.*

RK, Mandeville, LA

A: Did he confess to your girlfriend because he wanted you to find out about his crush . . . or because he just needed to tell someone how he felt? Either way, he didn't tell you himself, which probably means that he's not ready to do anything about his feelings. Also, do you want to tell him that you know and talk it over friend to friend, or do you want to pretend that you don't know, which might lead you to act differently around him? Think about him, think about you, and come to a decision that works for the both of you.

Q: *A good guy friend has a new girlfriend who hates me. She thinks I'm trying to steal him away (which I'm totally not). So what do I do?*

TS, Westtown, NY

A: She's probably just insecure about the two of you. How about including her in your friendship with her boyfriend? Once she gets to know you better, she'll understand that you're just her guy's bud.

DEAR JENNY

Q: *I heard that a guy in my English class likes me, but I don't like him that way. He's really cool and nice, but he's not hot at all. I know personality is supposed to be much more important, so why am I hung up on his not-so-cute looks?*

KP, Huntington Beach, CA

A: Don't worry—just because you're not interested in him that way doesn't mean you're superficial. There's a little something called chemistry that just might not be there between you two. The great thing, though, is that chemistry can definitely develop once you start getting to know someone better!

Q: *My boyfriend's friends don't like me. When Tim and I hang out with them, hardly any of them will even talk to me. They seem annoyed that I'm even there. How can I win them over?*

MS, Fair Lawn, NJ

A: Well, they could be a little jealous that they don't have girlfriends, and they could be a little jealous that you're taking their bud away from them, or they could just need some time to get to know you. Give them a little time to get used to you. You'll be one of the guys before you know it.

Do you have any questions about love?
Although we can't respond individually to your letters,
you just might find your questions answered in our column.

Write to:
Jenny Burgess or Jake Korman
c/o 17th Street Productions,
an Alloy Online, Inc. company.
33 West 17th Street
New York, NY 10011

Don't miss any of the books in *Love Stories*
—the romantic series from Bantam Books!